EVE -

BOOK TWO - THE SABELA SERIES

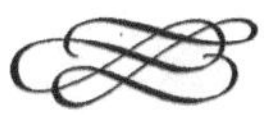

TINA HOGAN GRANT

CHAPTER 1

SABELA

$\mathcal{I}$ couldn't wait until I was home so I could tell my mom, Charlotte, her only daughter was finally getting married. The minute Slater asked me, I thought of my dad, wishing he was still with us to give me away. I can't believe it's been almost three years since he unexpectedly passed away from a heart attack at the young age of fifty-one, leaving my mom a widow at forty-nine, and me without a father at twenty-three.

Ever since that horrible day, I've stayed close to my mom, living in the San Diego area. In fact, Slater and I have been staying with her for the past eight months. That was when my ex, Davin, snapped and began stalking me. He tried to rape me; thank god Slater walked in and stopped him by beating the crap out of him. Turns out, he also raped two other women at the University of Texas where he was enrolled. After an emotional trial, he got what he deserved and is now spending fifteen years behind bars.

I met Slater on the beach the day Davin and I went our separate ways. I had gone there to try and get myself out of my depressed state after we said goodbye at the airport. Slater was the cure for that. It was an instant attraction that I couldn't, and didn't want to, fight.

He was my rock during those difficult times. I don't know what I would have done without him. He stuck by me through all of Davin's demented ways, when most guys would have run in the opposite direction. Now, we've been dating for a year and a half. Some may think we're rushing into things by getting married so soon, but when you know it's right, you just go with it. That's how I feel about Slater. God, I love him so much and now, he's asked me to be his wife.

After Slater proposed to me on the beach, I couldn't stop myself from jumping up and down in the sand like a silly little girl. I wanted to rush to my mom's and tell her the fantastic news.

"Come on, Slater, let's go home." I squealed and pulled on his hand, trying to yank him up from where he sat cross-legged on the towel.

"Hold on a second." He laughed. "I need to recuperate from our wild sex on the beach session that we've just had while strangers looked on."

I felt my cheeks warm at the mention of the sexual fetish we had discovered together. Yes, Slater and I liked to be watched while having sex. It was our little secret and we found it so liberating. I never knew what such a turn-on it could be until it accidentally happened the first day we met.

It's only happened on the beach, and then there was one time at work, which we quickly learned wasn't a good idea, and have refrained from letting that happen again. No words were exchanged with our audience. We didn't even know their names. It was better that way. The only person touching me was Slater, but the rush I felt, knowing the other guys were wishing they were Slater, was mind-blowing. No one got harmed or was forced to do anything they didn't want to do. Slater and I also had a signal—if I felt uncomfortable at all, I just pinched the tip of his nose and he would end it. So far, I hadn't had a problem and I never had to pinch his nose. I'd just been having too much fun with our new game. Everyone left with a smile on their face and a head full of erotic images to last until the next time.

"Come on, Slater!" I snickered impatiently. "We have so much to talk about and plan. First thing we have to do is set a date," I said, with wide eyes and a large grin as I continued to pull on his hand.

"Okay. Okay, I'm coming," he said, taking my hand and pulling himself up. Once on his feet, he wrapped me in his arms and gave me a loving squeeze around my waist. "Come here and give me a kiss, beautiful."

I let out a giggle and met his soft lips. His breath tasted fresh from the salt that lingered from his earlier surfing session. We kissed passionately for a few minutes, exploring each other's tongues and fondling one another's bodies in places that were meant to be aroused, until I forced myself to break away. "Come *on*, Slater. It's time to go," I said, panting, my palms resting on his bare chest.

"I know. I just can't get enough of you," he said before stealing another kiss. "Let me grab my gear and we're out of here."

Keeping our distance to avoid any more temptations, I quickly got dressed in my shorts and top while Slater threw on his jeans and t-shirt, then grabbed his surfboard. I carried his wetsuit and the remainder of our stuff.

It took us about twenty minutes to drive to my mom's house. For Slater, it was probably the longest twenty minutes he'd ever known. I couldn't stop talking or shifting in my seat, between ideas for the wedding and how anxious I was to see my mom's face once we told her.

As soon as we pulled into the driveway, I leapt out of the truck and raced around to the driver's side. I swung open the door and, wasting no time, grabbed Slater's hand and began pulling him out of the truck before he had a chance to take the keys out of the ignition. "Come on, I can't wait! Leave our stuff here. We can get it later," I said anxiously, still pulling on his hand.

Slater laughed at my enthusiasm and quickly jumped out to join me, pocketing his keys. Still holding his hand, I practically dragged him through the front door and began yelling for my mom. "Mom! Mom! We're home. Where are you?"

A few seconds later, she appeared in the doorway of the kitchen, holding a dishtowel. "Sabela. Are you okay? Why all the noise?" she asked, wearing a concerned look.

With my adrenaline leading me, I left Slater standing in the doorway and raced over to her and took the towel from her hands. "Mom. Come sit down. We have something to tell you," I said, walking her over to the dining room table.

Confusion blanketed her face, but without a fuss, she did as I asked and took a seat. I could tell my mother wasn't worried. The smile that beamed across my face told her it was good news.

"Well?" my mother asked in a surprisingly patient voice, once we were all seated.

Reaching across the table, I squeezed her hand tight while Slater smiled and hooked his arm over my shoulder. With my eyes now misty, I squeezed her hand again—only this time, a little tighter. "Mom, were getting married!" I squealed.

Tears flooded my mom's eyes as she released a loud cry of happiness, before holding her hands up to her mouth. "Oh my goodness! I'm so happy!" she screamed, tears now streaming down her face.

I laughed between my own tears and handed her a tissue from the box on the table, then grabbed one for myself.

After wiping her eyes, she held my hand and gave Slater a loving smile. "I'm so excited. We have a wedding to plan," she said, still dabbing the remainder of her tears.

Overjoyed by her reaction to the news, I chuckled. "I know! But we have to set a date first." I turned and threw Slater a smile.

"There's so much to think about. But yes, soon we'll be planning the wedding."

Keeping his arm over my shoulder, Slater took my mom's hand in his other one. With a killer smile that warmed my heart, he looked at me and then at my mom, still holding his genuine smile. "Thank you for raising a beautiful daughter. I love her so much, and I promise you I will take good care of her, as best I know how."

Feeling like the luckiest woman on the planet, tears began to flood my eyes again. Seeing my drenched cheeks, Slater pulled me in and whispered, "I love you."

"I love you too," I whispered back.

My mom began to cry again after hearing Slater's promise. I reached across the table and handed her another tissue.

"Slater, you already do take care of her. I've never seen her so happy," she said while giving her face a final dab with the tissue, then gave him a warm smile. "Welcome to the family."

CHAPTER 2

SLATER

When I asked Sabela to marry me almost three months ago, she made my world complete when she said yes. I wanted nothing more than to spend the rest of my life with her and maybe I was getting ahead of myself, but I couldn't wait until we had a couple of kids running around.

We hadn't set a date yet but now that life was finally getting back to normal, we hoped to soon. But with the sudden announcement of a wedding on the horizon, we suddenly found ourselves overwhelmed with a long list of things to do.

Our number-one priority had been to get our own place and figure out how we were going to make money when the job at the condos wrapped up. We'd been lucky the worked dragged out for a few extra months because of permit issues, but we both knew it would eventually come to an end. While living with Charlotte we saved quite a bit of money, we ended up renting our own condo just over two months ago.

It was hard to leave Charlotte, but we didn't move too far, just a few miles away, into a two-bedroom condo that was within walking distance of the beach. The best thing was that Sabela still saw her mom at least three times a week.

Just as we suspected, the job at the site wrapped up shortly before we moved into the condo. So, Sabela and I took the plunge and started our own construction company, which we named S & S construction, and so far, it was working out great.

We were using the second bedroom as our office, which was Sabela's department. She handled the calls, scheduled the estimate appointments, and had done a good job advertising the business online and around town in the local newspapers. Since we started this adventure, we'd been lucky enough to have steady work most weeks, consisting of remodels, painting, laying floors, and whatever else we could handle. Drew had been a lot of help by throwing small jobs our way, and even selling us some bitching tools for cheap.

Jill's boyfriend, Travis, had also been great. Jill and Sabela used to work at the dental office together—Jill still worked there but even though Sabela didn't, they'd stayed in touch by meeting for lunch sometimes or, on many occasions, we'd all hook up for a game of pool in one of the nearby bars. Travis also worked in construction and had been sending people our way. I told him if I ever got a big job, I'd return the favor.

The jobs we'd been getting had been relatively small, where Sabela and I could handle them on our own. The pay wasn't great, but we were managing to barely scrape by and get the bills paid. What we needed is one big job that would keep us busy for a while and we could put some savings back in the bank. Until then, no wedding date would be set until we knew we could afford it. But Sabela was still making little plans and getting organized for when the big day arrives.

Today, we were wrapping up a bathroom floor installation consisting of tile and Sabela had left early to pay some bills and return customer calls. She also wanted to confirm the start of our new job tomorrow, which was gutting a kitchen and installing new cabinets, counter, a back splash, and a new tiled floor. If it was scheduled as planned, Sabela reminded me we needed to make a trip to Home Depot tonight to stock up on supplies and check on the order of the new cabinets. I loved how she kept me on track.

After finishing the tile job, I returned home in the late afternoon to find Sabela sitting on the couch, making another one of her lists. After closing the door, I tossed my tool bag on the bench along the wall and joined her. "Hey, beautiful. What are you working on?" I asked before giving her a peck on the cheek.

She looked up, boasting her radiant smile that never failed to melt my heart. "Our guest list for the wedding," she said, beaming.

"So soon?" I chuckled at her enthusiasm. "We don't even have a date yet."

"I know, but I don't want to leave everything to the last minute." She prodded my chest with two of her fingers. "That's when mistakes happen, and we may forget to invite people." She leaned back against the couch and looked up toward the ceiling. "Gosh, I wish my dad was here," she said, unable to hide the sudden sadness she felt.

I gave her shoulder an affectionate rub. "I know, sweetheart. I would love to have met him."

She pulled her focus away from the ceiling and positioned her body in a comfortable position, where she was facing me with one foot tucked up under her knee and her arm bent, resting on the back of the couch, supporting her head. "Who's going to give me away?" she asked in a solemn voice.

I didn't have an answer and simply shrugged my shoulders, unsure of what to say.

I watched as she pondered for a moment, deep in thought. Then, in a flash, she sat up, her back straight and eyes wide. She reached over and squeezed my thigh. "Do you think your dad will?" She didn't wait for an answer. "I've never met your parents,

Slater. In fact, come to think of it, we've never talked about them." She rubbed my thigh again and I took her hand in mine, gently kissing it—knowing the big question was coming next. "They *will* be coming to the wedding, won't they?"

And there it was. The question I had been dreading and now had to answer. I didn't speak right away. I didn't know what to say and sat silent for longer than I had intended.

"Slater?" Sabela asked, her eyes narrowed.

I looked down at her hand and tickled her palm with my fingertips as I spoke. "I'm sorry. No, they won't be coming to the wedding."

"What?" She shook our hands that were still entwined. "Slater, look at me."

I looked up and gave her a blank stare, unable to smile for her.

Sabela narrowed her eyes even more, causing her brow to crease. "Why not? Don't you get along with them?"

I wasn't ready to answer and remained silent.

She squeezed my hand. "I don't mean to pry, Slater. But if that's the case, maybe you guys can make amends before the wedding." She tilted her head so her eyes were level with mine. "I would love to meet them."

I shied away from her stare and looked down at our hands tangled together. I hadn't talked about my parents since I was six. I had no reason to. I had no other siblings, and now I didn't even remember what my parents looked like. They were a distant memory. Two people I never got to know.

For the first time since that horrible day, so long ago, my eyes became misty as I finally raised my head and met Sabela's stare. I struggled to speak clearly and hesitated between sentences. "They're dead, Sabela. They died in a car crash when I was six."

Sabela gasped and raised a hand to her mouth in disbelief. "Oh, I'm so sorry. I had no idea."

I squeezed her hand. "It's okay. How could you know. I've never told you because I don't like to talk about it."

"I'm so sorry," Sabela said again. "You don't have to tell me if you don't want to."

"No, it's okay. You should know." I managed to crack a smile. "After all, I *am* going to be your husband."

She gave me a warm smile but said nothing, simply waited for me to continue.

"I never knew my parents and have very few memories of them." I paused. "I was raised by my grandparents on my mother's side, just north of Sacramento. They did the best they could, but they had just lost their daughter and apparently, I'm the splitting image of my mother, which they kept reminding me of. They never got over the death of my mother and both became raging alcoholics, drowning their sorrows in liquor."

"Oh no," Sabela said, listening intently to my story.

"Most of the time, I had to fend for myself, cooking my own meals, doing my own laundry and walking myself two miles to school and back. I grew up really fast and began taking on small jobs at the young age of twelve. As soon as I could, I moved out of the house, left town, and moved in with my high school sweetheart, Eve." I looked away for a moment before looking at her again. "But that's another story that I don't want to talk about. Maybe another time, I'll fill you in on Eve."

Sabela let go of my hand and wrapped her arms around me before giving me a tender kiss on the lips. "Oh, Slater, no wonder you've never talked about your parents. How could you? You had a rough childhood." She hesitated for a moment. "Are your grandparents still alive?"

"I doubt it. They were in their sixties when they took me in almost twenty-three years ago. I'm sure the alcohol must have killed them by now. I never went back, and I've not kept in touch with them." I shrugged my shoulders. "I've had no reason to. As far as I know, I have no other family. My dad's parents died when he was young, and he never spoke about them. You are my only family, Sabela, and that's all I need." I cupped her face and kissed her. "I love you."

"I love you too, Slater. We'll make our own family and our own memories. As for this Eve you mentioned, I sense it didn't end well." Sabela patted my knee. "I don't need to know anything. Only tell me if you want to. What matters now is us."

I released a small laugh, thankful she didn't want to know more. "Thanks. I'll keep that in mind. Someday, I'll tell you. I promise. But one heartache is enough for now." I wanted to quickly change the subject from me and brought up another matter that had me concerned. "So, how'd it go with the bills? Are we going to make rent this month?"

Sabela laughed sarcastically. "Barely. Our savings have dwindled a lot this month because of the second truck we bought for me. I thought we were going to be okay for two months, but that's not the case. But I may have to sell my body to make next month's rent."

"Ooh, can I watch?" I joked.

"Ha! How about we charge people to watch us have sex," she said, followed by an outburst of laughter.

My eyes grew wide. "That's not a bad idea!"

"Slater, I was joking!" she squealed before slapping my thigh.

I gave her a devious smile. "You actually might be on to something," I said, followed by a snarky laugh. "I mean, think about it. We let people watch us for free on the beach and it totally turns us on. If we can charge for it, why shouldn't we?"

Sabela looked stunned. "Now, hold on a second. I wasn't being serious. And besides, isn't that prostitution?"

"I'm your fiancé. How is having sex with your fiancé prostitution? No one else will be having sex with you."

Sabela raised her voice a notch. "Okay, you're freaking me out. Let's drop this conversation."

"Not so fast, beautiful." Turned on by the idea, I inched my way closer to her and whispered in her ear, "Think about it. We'd be getting paid to do what we love to do. Which is making love to each other. And someone would be right there, watching us." I nibbled on her ear and ran my hand across the light silk material of the robe covering her thigh. "Not twenty feet away on the beach, but in the same room. We'd be up close and personal. They would see everything."

Sabela let out a faint gasp and leaned her head back while I caressed her neck with my tongue. "Go on," she murmured.

Knowing I had her attention, I continued with my fantasy. "The person would probably be sitting on a chair, naked, facing the bed." I slid my hand into the opening of her robe at her thighs and gently brushed the material aside, exposing the softness of her skin. She leaned back against the couch while gripping the carpet with her toes. As I spoke, I began to knead her thigh with deep long strokes. "While the person watched, I'd lead you over to the bed and stand you before me, where I would slowly undress you, while caressing every inch of your immaculate body."

Sabela's breathing began to intensify as she listened to my seductive speech. I continued to massage her thigh while covering her neck with sensual light kisses. I had her under my spell and gently pushed her legs apart with my hand. Welcoming my touch, she spread them a little further, allowing me to reach up and fondle her now moist silk panties. I breathed heavily over her lips. "They'd watch me kiss you passionately, exploring your mouth with my tongue." I leaned in and gave Sabela a hard kiss. She gasped again, louder this time, as I pulled away.

"I would then work my hungry lips down to your beautiful breasts." I slowly moved my head down to her heaving chest while untying her robe. With a few tugs on the belt, it easily came loose and I pulled it way from her glorious body, spreading it open like a pair of wings. "God, you're so beautiful." I moaned before latching on to one of her bare breasts while massaging her deeply between her legs. "I would talk to our audience. I would tell them to look at your stunning body, and I'd tell them how good your breasts taste in my mouth and feel in my hand."

Sabela had now joined me in my fantasy and grabbed chunks of my hair as I fed on her bosom and circled her nipples with my tongue.

"Oh, god, that feels so good, Slater." She whimpered and pulled my head closer to her chest. "I want our friend to watch you caress my breasts hard while biting my nipples."

I obliged her request and took a nipple between my teeth, and gave it a slight nip.

"Harder!" she cried.

"Oh, our friend would like it if you told me what you wanted," I whispered before giving her nipple an extra fierce nip.

"Oh, yes! Just like that. Do it again." Sabela panted while pushing her chest out further to meet my forceful bites.

Feeling her body melt beneath me and hearing her pounding heart as she continued to breathe at an accelerated rate, I bit down harder on her nipples and rubbed vigorously in a circular motion between her legs, causing her to grind hard against my hand. "While I'm undressing you, I'd work my way down to your moist spot, where our new friend would watch with envy as I spread your legs apart and tasted your succulent juices."

Sabela let out another moan as she continued to grind her body on the couch. "Oh, god, yes. I want you to taste me."

I released my mouth from her nipple and followed the contour of her abs with sensual kisses and wet strokes using my tongue until I had reached her sacred spot. Not missing a beat, I slowly pulled her panties down over her legs and past her feet. "Spread your legs for me," I ordered.

Anticipating my touch, Sabela quickly opened her legs and released a loud moan of pleasure when the warmth of my tongue began to tease her. "God, you taste so good," I mumbled in between licks. "I would be sure to tell our audience how good you taste. He would probably be playing with himself right about now. Does that turn you on?"

Sabela took her breasts in her hands and squeezed them hard, pushing them together while tantalizing her nipples with her fingers. "Yes, it does."

I spread her legs wider. "I would make sure he gets a good view of me licking you by spreading your legs wide. I would stop for just a second and turn to him, and I would ask him if he wants to watch me fuck you." I lick her again, sticking my tongue deep inside of her. "Would you like that?"

Sabela shook her head from side to side while squeezing her breasts harder. "Yes! I would!" she screamed.

I knew she was ready for me as much as I was aching for her. With one swift movement, I rose to my knees and pushed my stiff erection inside of her as I pulled her by the hips toward me. Sabela released a loud moan of satisfaction as I plunged deep inside of her. I met her moan and began thrusting my hips in a rhythmic motion, gaining speed with every push.

"Our audience would watch me, pounding deep inside of you while he masturbated himself to an orgasm." I groaned while bringing myself over the edge. With one final thrust, I buried myself deep inside of Sabela as the orgasm ripped through my entire body. A few seconds later, she let out a loud scream as her body descended into orgasmic jolts followed by short, sharp breaths.

"Holy fuck!" she said, her chest heaving. "Where the fuck did that come from? That was friggin' wild."

Still trying to catch my breath with my head resting on her stomach, I chuckled at her comment. "That was such a turn on. Imagine if we really did such a thing. It could be even wilder." I laughed while rising to my feet.

Sabela sat up and pulled her robe closed. "I never thought about taking our little fetish to the next level. But damn, you had me so turned on with your little fantasy, it might actually be fun."

She snickered before giving me a serious look. "As long as they don't touch me. That's a big no."

"Trust me, the only person that gets to touch you—and be inside of you, I might add—is me."

I wasn't sure how serious Sabela was about acting out the fantasy I had just created, but it had me thinking. It would be a great way to relieve some of our money pressures until the construction business got off the ground. But I wondered if Sabela was right and it was a form of prostitution. My curiosity had been piqued. The way we were both turned on and came so quickly had me wanting to consider the idea some more.

"If it's anything like we just played out in our minds, I think it would be kinda fun," I said with a smirk. "Can you imagine getting paid to have sex with one another." I took her in my arms and eased back against the couch, enjoying the feel of her head on my chest. "Do people actually do such a thing?"

Sabela laughed. "I can't believe we're even contemplating this idea of yours. But I bet there are couples that do it."

I looked down and gave her a light kiss on the top of her head. "I'm going to see what I can find out. God knows where I'll begin; there's not really anyone I can ask."

Sabela chuckled. "Look online. You can find anything online."

"Good idea."

"I'll even look with you."

Sabela snickered, and I was surprised by her enthusiasm. "You're really into this, aren't you?"

"I think it will be fun. I love being watched." She shrugged her shoulders in a carefree manner. "So, why not?"

"Okay then. We'll see what we can find out." I shifted in my seat and Sabela sat up. "In the meantime, are we starting that kitchen remodel tomorrow? If we are, then we still need to go to Home Depot tonight."

"Yep, we sure are. I talked to the husband, Mike, this afternoon, and it's a go. They're expecting us at eight in the morning. And I also got a message from a lady who is looking to hire someone. I called her back and left her a message. She hasn't called back yet."

"Great! Well, looks like we've got some worked lined up." I glanced at my phone sitting on the coffee table. "Okay, let's get dressed and get out of here. We've got a busy day tomorrow." I leaned in and squeezed her hard. "You're such a distraction."

Sabela laughed. "You're the one that came home with some wild fantasy. It's all your fault." She rose from the couch. "I'm going to get dressed."

I smacked her behind as she squeezed by me. "Make it quick."

CHAPTER 3

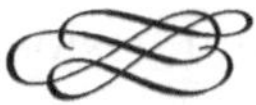

SABELA

I wasn't sure if Slater was serious about doing a live sex show in front of someone for money. But it sure was fun fantasizing about it on the couch with him a little while ago. He had me totally turned on. I'd be up to it. But I'll let him pursue it. I don't want to come across as too eager. Call me sexist, but it's better if the man takes charge in such situations.

In a mad dash to get dressed, I threw on the first pair of jeans I could find, a comfortable sweatshirt, and a pair of sneakers. I gave my hair a quick comb through and grabbed the file from the office for the kitchen remodel. In ten minutes, we were on the road to Home Depot.

After getting everything squared away at the store, we decided to stop and get a bite to eat at a local hamburger joint. While we were eating, Slater began surfing his phone. "Look at this. There *is* such a thing."

I took his phone and glanced down at the screen, so I could scan the ads. They were all for live sex shows by couples. "Well, I'll be damned," I said, as I continued to scroll down the screen. There must have been at least twenty of them. Many of the couples were naked, cute, and anywhere from their twenties to fifties. "It doesn't say how much they charge."

Slater took the phone back and did some searching of his own. "I'm sure you have to be a member of these sites to get that kind of information, and there's a fee, I'm sure, which I don't want to pay."

"No, I don't want this costing us money," I agreed, shaking my head. "That's not the plan. And besides, we can't afford it." Then I had an idea. "Wait! There's that newspaper, *LA Weekly*. I've seen all kinds of sex stuff advertised in that. I bet they have a website, and it's probably free." I grabbed my phone and began a search. A few minutes later, I found the site and began surfing it. "Yep, here you go," I said, and continued to read. "Live sex shows. And look, they even list San Diego."

Slater took my phone. "We should call one," he said, not taking his eyes off the screen. "Here's a couple that charges two hundred dollars an hour." He gasped. "Wow! It takes me half a day to make that much. It says we have to sign up to access their email."

I couldn't hide my elevated tone in my voice—I was shocked. "Slater! This began as an idea to make some extra cash, not spend it. We can't afford $200.00," I shrieked. "And besides, I'm not into watching another couple having sex. I think you've got this all backwards."

Slater laughed at my outburst and gave my knee a reassuring pat. "I don't want to watch them either. But if I email them, I can get an idea on what they say to potential customers. I have no idea what to say to anyone." He laughed. "Call this research."

Now he was making sense. "Oh okay. I gotcha," I said with a nod. "That's a damn good idea." I retrieved my phone from his hands and gave him a devious smile. "Well, let's go home and send some emails."

I must admit, the more we talked about it, the more excited I found myself becoming. I wasn't sure if I was more into it than

Slater, but I liked how naughty it was making me feel and, to be honest, I was kind of excited about getting home and checking out some of these couples online.

Once we were back at our condo, I quickly changed into my bathrobe and joined Slater on the couch, where we cuddled and scanned our phones. I wasn't interested in meeting any of these couples, but I was curious, like Slater was, on how they went about setting the whole thing up.

After a few minutes, Slater showed me a picture of a couple on his screen. I took the phone to get a closer look. They were about our age, in their mid-twenties. She had long, straight black hair and was wearing super-tight white shorts and a lacy white bra, while the guy was wearing tight jeans and no top. Their skin was tanned a deep dark bronze and they both looked like they were in good shape. "What do you think?" Slater asked.

"Shoot them email. Here's another couple." I handed him my phone, which had a picture of a slightly older couple, who were probably in their thirties. Both had blondish hair and were also in excellent shape.

After scanning the ads for the next half hour, Slater had a list of five couples he wanted to email. Between our giggles and disbelief that we were doing this, he sent all of them a quick message, inquiring about their services. "Okay. Now all's we have to do is wait to see if anyone replies," Slater said before turning off his phone and leaning back into the cushions of the couch.

"And if they do? I have no desire to meet these people or watch them have sex," I stated in a slightly raised tone, fearing Slater had other ideas.

Slater rubbed my thigh. "Don't worry. That's not why I'm doing this. I'm just going to ask them a bunch of questions and see what they tell me." He stroked my thigh again. "I'm only pretending I'm interested. Okay?"

I nodded. "Okay."

Once he had hit the send button, it suddenly felt so surreal and I began to question myself. The fantasies Slater and I shared were fantastic, but would the real thing be just as exciting? In our minds, we could create any situation we wanted to, and add whatever emotions we wanted to feel, but in real life, it would be raw and I'd have no control over my emotions.

On the beach, our audience wasn't close and we had absolutely no contact or any kind of conversation with them. I loved the anonymity of it all, but doing the live sex show thing would be completely different. We would be in the same room and we'd be talking to them. Suddenly, I began to think this wasn't such a good idea after all.

Slater must have seen me deep in thought because he gave me a friendly nudge. "Hey, are you okay?" he asked, leaning in and wrapping his arm around me.

I tucked my head under his chin, breathing in his scent. "Yeah, I'm good. Just some silly stuff going through my head."

"Well, tell me about it," he said with a look of concern.

"Oh, it's nothing. I just hope the real thing is as good as our fantasy."

Slater rubbed my shoulder and pulled me in closer. "Listen, if you don't want to do this, it's fine with me. This is supposed to be fun and we both have to enjoy it." He paused for a second. "If it's the money part that bothers you, well, hell, we don't have to charge. I was just making a joke." He chuckled and gave my shoulders another rub. "We'll get by. To be honest, I would feel kind of weird taking money from someone for doing what we love to do."

I laughed at his confession and gave him a slap on the knee. "Isn't that why we got into this? Because we needed the money," I joked. "But now that you mention it, it would make me feel kind of cheap." I didn't need to think about what I wanted to say next. I realized now, part of my problem was the money thing, but didn't realize it until Slater pointed it out. "Yeah, let's leave the money out of it. I'd feel so much better."

Feeling excited about this new possible adventure we might explore, I glanced at my phone and saw it was almost eleven. "Come on, let's go to bed. We've got a busy day tomorrow." I pulled myself away from his arm and squeezed his side. "We can talk more about this under the covers," I said, followed by a playful wink.

CHAPTER 4

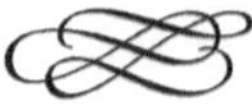

SLATER

It ended up being a late night for Sabela and me. The sex was wild as we once again shared our fantasies of what may happen if we placed an ad for a live sex show. I gotta say though, whether we go through with it or not, the idea is certainly adding to our sex life. We both keep talking about it and when we do, within a few minutes, we're fucking each other's brains out.

The next morning, we were both dragging our feet, and I was relieved we had made the Home Depot run last night, thanks to Sabela's suggestion. Both trucks were loaded with supplies and by seven thirty, we were out the door. Our plan was to demo as much of the kitchen by noon before the new cabinets were due to be delivered.

When we arrived, we were greeted by Mike, the owner of the house, who was standing on his front porch, looking sharp in his navy-blue suit. "Right on time," he said, glancing at his watch with a satisfactory smile as I stepped out of my truck.

"Only way I roll," I replied as I waited for Sabela to park behind me and join us.

Drew, who currently had his crew working on a strip mall, had referred us to Mike. We'd gone over the plans with Mike a few weeks ago, and he was adamant the job be completed within seven days because it was his wife's birthday and they had a big birthday bash planned at the house. This was a good paying job Sabela and I needed to see us through the next month, and I promised Mike it would be done. Now, the pressure was on. But Sabela and I worked good together and, without a doubt, I knew we wouldn't fail him.

I was guessing Mike was probably in his late fifties. During our conversations, he told me him and his wife had been married for almost thirty years and had three kids. Two sons and a daughter, and they were expecting their first grandchild in two months. He also told me he'd worked in car sales his entire life and his wife was a nurse. Their home was a typical family-sized home, with three bedrooms and two baths, and they had future plans to remodel the bathrooms. Using a firm handshake, he had said if we did a good job on the kitchen, he would hire us to do the task.

As soon as Sabela stepped out of her truck, I was reminded what a lucky man I was. Every time I looked at her, she never failed to tickle my heart. I extended my arm to greet her, admiring the way she looked in her tight-hugging blue jeans, white t-shirt, and work boots. "Mike, you remember my fiancée, Sabela," I said, wrapping my arm around her waist.

Mike walked down the path from his front door, his briefcase in hand, and shook Sabela's hand. "I sure do," he replied with a smile.

"Hi, Mike. Good to see you again," Sabela said, in her sweetest, most professional voice.

"Well, the house is all yours. Nancy, my wife, has already left for the day, and I'm out the door. "

"Okay. Sounds good," I said.

We stood in the path, as Mike gave us some more instructions. "I left a key on the counter, in case you need to step out. Take it with you when you leave, so you can lock up."

I nodded. "Sure. Not a problem."

Mike extended his hand. "Thanks again. Neither one of us will be home until after seven. If you have any questions, feel free to call me anytime."

"You got it, Mike," I said, shaking his hand.

Once Mike left, we wasted no time unloading the trucks and getting organized for the demo. We were pleased to see all the cabinets had been emptied prior to our arrival, and their contents packed in boxes that were neatly stacked in the dining room. That job alone would have cost us a few hours of work. With everything in place, we were ready to begin.

Sabela was looking as cute as ever, with her tool belt hanging from her waist. We dove right in and had the kitchen completely gutted within a few hours, and I was feeling confident we would have the job finished by the end of the week.

The new cabinets were delivered right on time, and I had the delivery crew stack them on the floor in the middle of the spacious kitchen. Sabela helped me figure out the measurements for the first cabinet but when it was time to lift it and hold it against the wall, I saw her struggling.

"Are you okay?" I asked as she leaned her body tight against the wall, trying to support the cabinet up high.

"Yeah, but these are really heavy. I'm strong, but not that strong," she complained.

"Here, let's put it down. I don't want you to hurt yourself," I said, concerned Sabela may get injured. This was our first cabinet installation, and I wasn't sure if Sabela could handle the weight of the upper cabinets. It took a lot of upper strength to hold one of them up while the other person screwed it to the wall. "I don't think you're strong enough to do this part of the job, Sabela. I don't want you to get hurt."

"Well, we really don't have a choice. It's just you and me, babe."

I thought for a moment. "You know, this job is paying us pretty well. We can afford to hire a third hand for the heavy lifting parts. What do you say?"

"I'm game," she said, rubbing her back. "My back is already starting to hurt. But who do you have in mind?'

"I could ask Travis. Last time I talked to him, he said work had been slow. Let me give him a call right now." I pulled out a chair. "Here, come take a break."

"Gladly," Sabela said, grabbing a bottle of water from the ice chest, then taking a seat.

I left her alone while she browsed her phone, and went outside to call Travis. After a few rings, he answered the call in a sharp tone. "Travis speaking."

"Hey, Travis, it's Slater. Everything okay? I didn't catch you at a bad time, did I?" I asked cautiously.

"Nah. Jill and I are just going through a rough patch right now. What's up?"

"Oh, I'm sorry to hear that." I didn't want to pry and quickly changed the subject to the reason why I was calling. "Listen, I was wondering if you could use a little bit of work. Sabela and I are installing some cabinets, but she's having a hard time lifting them and we could really use your help, man."

Travis's voice suddenly carried a much happier tone. "Sure, your timing couldn't be any better. I'm wrapping up a job today. How about tomorrow morning?"

"That would be great!" I said, relieved. "Let me give you the address. We'll be here at eight, by the way."

After relaying the necessary information to Travis, I hung up the call and went back into the house. I figured Sabela and I could spend the day installing the lower cabinets and Travis could help me tomorrow with the upper ones.

I found Sabela still sitting but speaking to someone on the phone. She threw me a smile and raised her hand as if to say, "One minute." I understood and moved quietly around the kitchen until she was finished with her call.

"Who was that I?" I asked after she hung up.

She beamed. "That was Everleigh," she said, excitement shining in her eyes.

"Who?"

Sabela rolled her eyes at my forgetfulness. "The woman that I've been waiting for—to call me back about a job."

Suddenly, I remembered. "Oh, that woman. How did it go?"

"She sounds really nice over the phone and she may have a lot of work for us," Sabela said, standing. "I'll find out more tomorrow, if I'm able to leave here for a bit."

"I don't see why not."

"Hey, how did it go with Travis?" Sabela asked, putting her phone in the back pocket of her jeans.

I smiled. "Travis will be here bright and early in the morning to help with the upper cabinets."

Sabela clenched her fist while doing a little dance. "Yeah!"

"If you want, we can work on the lower ones today. So yes, go meet with Everleigh in the morning, and then come over here when you're done."

"Perfect!" Sabela put on her tool belt, then slapped my behind. "Okay, boss, so where do we start?"

The rest of the day went smoothly and we were able to get all the lower cabinets installed. By the time five o'clock rolled around, we had cleaned up our mess, packed away our tools, and were admiring our work.

"Damn, we do good work." I said, squeezing Sabela's waist.

Sabela twisted away from the tickle. "Yes, we do. I'm excited about meeting with Everleigh tomorrow. I got the impression she has a lot of work that needs to be done. She talked about her floors, the kitchen, the bathrooms, and painting." She pulled out a piece of paper from her pocket, unfolded it, and looked at it. "Her address is in Del Mar Heights. Isn't that a rich neighborhood?"

I took the piece of paper from her to double check the address.

"Yeah, it is. It's where all the doctors, lawyers, and actors live. She must have a pretty big house. Did she tell you how big it was?"

"No, I'll see it tomorrow. God, Slater, this job might be just what we need to get ahead. I'll do my best to get us the work."

Sabela was right. This sounded like it might be a huge job. If her instincts were correct, we might be living comfortably for a while. The thought brought a smile to my face. "Come on. Let me take you out to dinner. Call it a pre-celebration."

Sabela pressed her body against me and I wrapped my arms around her as she kissed me passionately. "I don't want to jinx it, but dinner does sound good."

CHAPTER 5

SABELA

Normally when I do estimates, I dress casual, in my normal attire of jeans and a t-shirt. For the estimate with Everleigh, I wanted to look more professional in the hopes of impressing her, so I took my time deciding what to wear. Slater had already left to go meet Travis at the job site, and my appointment with Everleigh wasn't until ten, which gave me plenty of time to be fussy. I decided on a black pair of pants and a thin grey sweater, along with a pair of black flats. I also remembered to pack some work clothes, so I could change when I got to Mike's house.

Driving through the streets of Del Mar Heights, I felt like a fish out of water. I had never been to this area before and I was blown away. Even after taking extra time to decide what to wear, I still felt underdressed. There was no doubt I was amongst the rich.

Luscious green lawn surrounded every elegant mansion, with palms trees standing tall along the streets and on the properties. Jaguars, Porches, and Mercedes were parked in the sprawling driveways. There was no traffic on the wide, perfectly manicured roads lined with hedges and flowerbeds.

As I drove through the neighborhood at a slower speed, I

gasped at the size of the houses, with their large entrance ways, large picture windows, and elegant lawn ornaments that probably cost more than I make in a year. Right about now, I wished I was driving a brand-new Ford pick-up and not my used 2010 white Chevy, which stood out like a sore thumb. While still in awe of my surroundings, my GPS on my phone told me to turn right onto a cul-de-sac, which I did, and within thirty seconds, I had reached my destination.

With the engine still running, I double-checked the address. Yes, this was it. "Wow," I said out loud.

I peered out through the passenger side window and found myself parked in front of a large, beautiful, white colonial house, surrounded by tall palm trees, an immaculate green lawn edged with ornate pots filled with yellow, white, and orange flowers. Off to the right, away from the house, was a three-car garage with a white Lexus parked in the driveway. The arched entranceway on the left led to double wooden doors, also decorated with ornate pots on either side.

Not wanting to drive my dirty old truck up on the spotless driveway—I would die if I left oil marks—I opted to stay on the street and turned off the engine. After giving my hair a quick shake and a comb with my fingers, I quickly applied some lipstick and grabbed my clipboard, wishing I had a briefcase instead. I checked myself one more time in the rearview mirror and retrieved my keys from the ignition. "Okay let's do this," I whispered under my breath.

Clutching my clipboard against my chest, with my purse hanging over my shoulder, I made my way up to the front door, all while admiring the grandeur of the house. *Damn, what do you have to do for a living to own this kind of home? Slater and I will never make enough to have something like this.*

When I finally reached the front door, I took in a deep breath before ringing the doorbell. A few minutes later, the door opened and to my surprise, a rather young woman answered the door. She must have been close to my age, in her mid to late twenties, unless she looked really good for her age. She was stunning and perfect in every way, from her long mane of golden blonde hair that flowed down her back to her perfectly formed body.

She was wearing tight, form-fitting black leggings that enhanced every curve of her legs. Her top was a sports bra, also black, and low-cut, which accentuated her large breasts. Her abs were clearly defined and her skin was deeply tanned and flawless. Suddenly, I felt like a plain Jane next to her and stuttered when I spoke.

"Hi. Err, Everleigh? I'm, err, Sabela. We had an appointment at ten." I checked my watch. It was five minutes before. "I'm not too early, am I?"

Everleigh opened the door wider, but not before peering over my shoulder. "No, not at all. Come on in." She motioned me in with her hand. "Perfect timing. My trainer won't be here for another hour." She paused for a moment while taking one more look past me. "Are you alone?"

"Yes. Slater, my fiancé, is busy today, so it's just me. Is that okay?"

I couldn't help noticing the look of disappointment that appeared on her face.

"Yes, that's fine. His name is Slater?" she asked, puzzled.

"Yes. Actually, that's his nickname. His real name is Ian. But no one ever calls him that anymore. He will probably make it to our next meeting if we have one."

"Ah, I see," Everleigh replied, replacing her look of disappointment with a smile.

I stepped into the large entranceway and couldn't help looking up at the large crystal chandelier above me. "Oh, that is gorgeous. You have a beautiful home."

Everleigh closed the door behind us as I stood grounded to my spot on the marbled floor, afraid to move. "Thanks, I've only been here a month. I just got out of a divorce and now reaping in my rewards." She laughed.

"Oh, I'm sorry."

She flipped her hand and shook her head. "Oh, don't be. I'm not." She laughed again. "I should never have married the asshole."

I was stunned by her language, but it broke the ice and made her seem more real.

She ushered me further into the house. "Come on, let me show you around."

"Should I take off my shoes?" I asked.

"Oh no, don't be silly. I have mainly marble and hardwood. You're fine. You're not wearing heels. That's what does the most damage."

Still clinging to my clipboard, I followed her through the house, afraid to touch any of the white painted walls for fear of leaving fingerprints. She led me to the main room first, which opened to a humongous kitchen, separated by an elegant granite island. The floors were wide plank hardwood, the walls a crisp white, and large picture windows with white wooden shutters lined the walls. The view of the ocean below was breathtaking, no matter where you looked. The kitchen was equipped with high-end stainless-steel appliances and ornate off-white cabinets. This room alone was probably bigger than the condo Slater and I lived in. Off from the kitchen were four glass doors that led out onto a huge deck and an outside kitchen, complete with a top-of-the-line barbecue area, a bar with stools, and oversized outdoor plush seating. A vast number of shrubs and flowers in flowers boxes and pots were placed sporadically throughout the seating area and against the wooden railings.

"This is just beautiful," I said, taking it all in.

"Thanks. Come on, let me show you the rest."

The rest of the house was just as grand as the main room. Every one of the five bedrooms and four bathrooms were immaculately furnished and decorated with exquisite taste I would probably never afford in my lifetime. Expensive rugs complemented the hardwood floors in every room. Each bathroom was ornate, with their marble counters and floors. Lush linens blanketed every bed and beautiful artwork hung from every wall.

"Your house is so amazing," I said, as we headed back to the main living area and took a seat at the kitchen bar, where Everleigh handed me a glass of chilled water. "It's perfect in every way. What could you possible need work on?"

Everleigh gave me a warm smile. "Thank you, but as I mentioned earlier, I've only been here for a month and everything you see in this house came with the purchase. I've not done a thing to the place." She took a sip of her water. "You see, I have a nephew that I adore, and he will be visiting me frequently once the work I'm requesting has been done." She glanced around the room while raising her hand. "But look around."

I scanned the room while she kept talking.

"This house is for grown-ups."

I nodded.

"I want to have a place especially for my nephew while he's here. I want him to have his own room, and one of the bathrooms would need to be kid-friendly too."

I nodded again, then reached for my clipboard and began taking notes.

"I want a fenced play area for him outside, with a sandbox, and a playground with bikes and lots of toys. The finished basement that I showed you, just sits empty. Let's make it into a little boy's haven, maybe build a movie theatre with a popcorn machine." She laughed.

I was moved by her admiration for her nephew. A child that wasn't even hers, and yet she wanted to give him so much. Maybe she couldn't have children and this was the child she never had. "I see. Wow! What a great aunt you are."

"He is my world. I count the days until he is with me again." She suddenly became serious. "Do you have children, Sabela?"

"No, I don't. Not yet anyhow. Slater and I want to have kids after we're married, but we haven't even set a date for our wedding yet."

Everleigh reached across the counter and took my hand, surprising me. "I bet you will make a great mother. I can tell you love children. What about Slater?"

"Oh, he wants them just as much as I do." Wanting to get off the subject of me, I quickly changed it back to her nephew. "So, where does your nephew live? Does he live far?"

"He and his mother—my sister—are living with our mother in Escondido, close to his pre-school. My dad passed when I was ten, from cancer, and now my sister is sick and needs help taking care of him."

"Oh, I'm so sorry. This must be a difficult time for you," I said with concern.

"It is, but my mother and I are helping as much as we can with the little one, which is why money is not an issue with the plans I have here. I want him to have everything a child could possibly want. I want him to forget about the troubles at home and just be a child when he's here. She paused for a moment. "Does that make sense?"

I could feel my eyes getting misty from her touching confession and discreetly gave them a wipe with my hand. "Yes, it does. I think what you are doing is beautiful. So, it's just you living here?" I asked, looking around the room again.

"Yes, it is. I like my space. It's going to be a surprise, so I won't have Scottie here until everything is completed. That's my nephew's name, by the way. It will be tough not having him here, but in the meantime, I'll just make more visits to my mom's house." Everleigh glanced at her watch. "I hate to end this. I love talking to you, but my trainer is due here any minute."

She took another sip of her water. "You've seen the house and I've told you what I want to have done, so what I'd like you to do is come up with a plan and present it to me in a few days. And remember, spare no expense." She threw me a large smile. "I like you and if you want it, the job is yours."

I was stunned and couldn't hide my excitement. "Really! I already have all kinds of ideas roaming around in my head. I won't disappoint you, I promise."

Everleigh laughed at my enthusiasm as she rose from her stool and approached me with an extended hand, which I took and shook vigorously.

"Thank you. I can't wait to get started. Shall I call you in a couple of days?" I said, standing.

Still laughing from my overabundance of excitement, she rested her hand on my shoulder as she led me to the front door. "That would be fine. I can't wait to hear what you've come up with. Now, I really must go, and thank you."

I shook her hand one last time before leaving and she closed the door behind me.

"*Yes!*" I squealed while jumping in the air, only to be startled by the loud crashing sound of my clipboard falling to the ground. Embarrassed she may have seen my clumsy act, I quickly scooped it up and raced to my truck to call Slater about the good news.

CHAPTER 6

I tried my best to concentrate on the job with Travis, but it was hard when I was wondering how Sabela was doing in her meeting. We had absolutely no idea how big the job was or if we'd even get it. But Sabela always looked at the glass half full and felt confident we would. "*She* called *us*, didn't she?" she reminded me last night. "We already have one foot in the door. I just need to cinch the deal. I know I can do this."

Those were her last words before I headed out the door. If she was right about this, life may be looking pretty damn good soon.

Travis and I worked all morning on the upper cabinets and had them installed by lunchtime. He had voluntarily shared the problems he was having at home and in confidence, told me he and Jill may be splitting up because he had met someone else. I tried to be a friend, to just listen and not be judgmental. I liked Jill and they'd been together for a few years. "Does Jill know?" I asked.

"No, not yet. You're the only person I've told."

The news made me uncomfortable. "Oh man, I wish you hadn't told me that," I said, shaking my head. "Don't you think you should have told Jill first? It's going to be really awkward if I see her." I let out a heavy sigh. "That's one hell of a secret you're asking me to keep."

Travis dug his fingers into his brown hair and scratched the top of his head vigorously. "I'm sorry, bro. I just needed to get it off my chest. I'm gonna tell her. Soon, I promise." He looked at me with pleading eyes. "I just need to figure all this out. Promise me, you won't tell Sabela. I know her and Jill are good friends."

"Are you sure you know what you're doing? Jill's a good woman. When we all had dinner a few weeks ago, you both seemed really happy. Don't rush into something and throw it all away, man," I said, feeling concerned.

"That was all a front, bro. Jill and I have not been getting along for a long time." He let out a sarcastic laugh. "Shit, we've not had sex in over six months. What does that tell you?"

I was stunned by his confession. "Fuck. I thought you guys were a good match."

Travis shook his head. "Nah, we've kind of grown apart. It's been over for a while. And now that I'm seeing someone else, it's time we faced the truth."

Against my better judgment, I agreed to keep the upsetting news to myself. I didn't agree with what Travis was doing, but I already knew too much and hoped he'd come clean with Jill soon. I didn't like holding secrets, especially from my fiancée.

After lunch and still no word from Sabela, we made a start on installing the plywood for the granite counter tops, which were due to be delivered in two days. After the first piece had been installed successfully, my phone rang and my heart skipped a beat when I saw it was Sabela. In haste, I tossed the tape measure to Travis. "Hey, I gotta take this call. It's Sabela. Grab the measurements for the next piece, I'll be right back."

"Sure, not a problem. I hope it's good news," he called as I headed out the front door.

With my heart still , I answered the phone. "Hey, babe. How'd it go?"

"We got the job, baby!" Sabela screamed into the phone, her voice reaching a high pitch of excitement.

I couldn't believe what I was hearing. "You're kidding? Seriously? The job is ours?"

"Yes! She hired us on the spot. You won't believe this place. And get this, she said money is not an issue. This woman is loaded." Sabela took a moment to catch her breath. "I'll tell you more when I get there. I'll see you soon. I love you."

"I love you too. Wow! This is unbelievable."

I ended the call and rushed back into the house. I couldn't wait to tell Travis. He knew right away from the humongous grin on my face that the news was good.

"You got the job, eh?" he said, before I had a chance to speak.

"We did. I can't believe it. I'm not sure what the job entails, but there may be some work for you in it. I'll let you know after Sabela fills me in."

A large grin appeared on Travis's face. "That would be cool, man. Thanks. Work's kinda slow right now, and I don't want to be hanging around the house."

~

Forty-five minutes later, the patter of feet could be heard running on the hardwood floors in the hallway. I heard the joyous voice of Sabela. "Slater, are you here?"

"Yes, in the kitchen," I hollered, setting my hammer down on the plywood counter we had just installed.

A few minutes later, she appeared in the doorway, wearing the biggest grin that instantly rubbed off on me. "Baby, can you believe it? This job is going to put us on easy street for a while. I'm so excited!" She squealed as she raced into my arms and hooked her arms around my neck, followed by an awesome passionate kiss.

When she eventually broke away, she noticed Travis off to the side at the two sawhorses, measuring a piece of plywood. "Hi, Travis. Sorry, I didn't see you there."

Travis turned around and gave Sabela a friendly nod. "Hey, Sabela. Well done on getting the job. That's great news."

"Thanks," she said before turning her attention back to me. With her arms still hooked around my neck, I held her tightly around the waist, enjoying the festive moment.

"So, tell me. What does this woman want us to do?" I asked.

"Well apparently, she has a young nephew whose mother is sick, so the little boy comes and stays with Everleigh frequently, and she wants us to do all kinds of things for him."

Sabela quickly explained what we would be doing. The basement alone could take some time, depending on what plans we come up with, and prepping and building an outside area would be at least a few weeks, if not more. She went on to tell me the bedroom and bathroom would need some work too. "This is frigging awesome!" I yelled as I swung her around in mid-air.

"I can't wait to get started. My mind is going crazy with a ton of ideas. She wants me to call her in a few days and show her what we've come up with. Do you need me here? I'd love to go home and get started on this."

"No. Travis and I have this covered. You know what a kid needs more than I do. Work your magic, beautiful. I'll see what you've come up with I get home."

Sabela grabbed her purse that had dropped to the ground amongst the excitement and swung it over her shoulder. "Great!" she said, before planting another kiss on my lips. "I'll see you at home." She turned and faced Travis. "Bye, Travis."

"Bye, Sabela."

I still couldn't believe it and shook my head. "Wow, this is friggin awesome. *And* the woman doesn't care what it cost." I turned to Travis. "Looks like I'll be needing you for a while, dude," I said with a large smile, knowing it was good news for Travis.

"Thanks man, I really appreciate it. I'll take you guys out for a game of pool soon."

For the remainder of the day, my spirits were the highest they've been in a long time, and I could feel the stresses of life beginning to ease up. I found myself thinking often about the wedding Sabela and I want so much. We hadn't talked much about it because we'd not had the money to plan one. *Maybe this job will make it happen?* Sabela deserved a nice wedding. She never complained when money was tight. She always seemed to see the lighter side of things and her favorite thing to say was, "We're in this together and we'll get by." God, I love her so much. Maybe it was time to finally set a wedding date. I think tonight I'm going to take her out for a celebration dinner and bring it up.

While Travis and I were wrapping it up for the day, my phone dinged with an incoming email. Wanting to make sure it wasn't a work-related emergency, I decided to check it before packing up my tools, and immediately took a seat when I saw it was from one of the couples we had emailed a few days ago. I waited anxiously for the email to load, and was startled when Travis came back into the kitchen. I quickly covered the screen of my phone with my hand.

"Do you need me tomorrow, man?" he asked as he grabbed his bag.

"I thought you'd left already," I answered in a surprised tone. "Yeah, as a matter of fact, I do. The countertops are now coming tomorrow, and are too heavy for Sabela to lift. Besides, she probably wants to stay home and write up some plans for the new job. It would be great if you could help install them."

"You got it, man. I'll see you in the morning."

After he had left, I quickly went back to the email.

· · ·

Hi guys,
    It's Susie and Vic. We'd love to put on a show for you. Give us a call. We hate this back and forth email stuff. Our number is 555-000-5555. Can't wait to hear from you.
    Love Susie & Vic. Xoxox

I had to read the letter a few times to let it sink in. I was stunned someone had replied to us. This was the older couple in their mid-thirties. "Now what?" I said out loud. Damn, Sabela and I are going to have lot to talk about tonight. I'd better get out of here.

CHAPTER 7

When I arrived home, I put aside all responsible chores I had planned on doing, such as laundry, dishes, and cooking dinner, and got right to work on my presentation for Everleigh. I rushed around the house like a mad woman, kicking off my shoes in the middle of the room, racing to the kitchen to make a hot cup of herbal tea. Within minutes, I was heading up to the office to jot down my ideas that had been spinning around in my head for hours, before I forgot them.

I figured a train theme would be good for Scottie's bedroom. What little boy doesn't like trains? I was sure we could find a bedframe that looked like one. Thank god for the internet. We could put a large train track and train around the entire perimeter of the room. Maybe even big enough for him to ride. His clothes and toys could be stored in lockers, like you'd find at the station. The room could be bright happy colors, like reds and blues. I also had some ideas about building a secret room, a slide, a reading area, and a game center. The finished basement would be the perfect place for a movie theatre and an area for more games and another slide. Maybe a ball pit, like they have in Chucky Cheese, and definitely some arcade games.

I'd have to talk with Slater about the outside area. We'd have to make sure the ground was perfectly flat and build a white picket fence to match the colonial design of the house. We could build a sandbox, a wading pool, outdoor swings, and slides. Oversize lawn games like candy cane and checkers would be fun too. A track for the power wheels that I intend to buy for the area would be awesome along with colorful benches and tables. I soon realized my list was huge, but Everleigh had said spare no expense.

As for the bathroom, that would be a simple makeover with kid-friendly colors and accessories. Right now, it was gold and white, and we could easily change it to blues and use a boat theme. Maybe I could even find an artist to paint a mural in each room. The idea excited me, and I jotted down design ideas for each room.

I'm not sure what time it was when I heard Slater announce his presence from downstairs. "Hey babe, I'm home. Where are you at?"

I'd been up in the office for hours and had obviously lost track of time. "I'm up in the office," I hollered while organizing my piles of notes. A few minutes later, I heard his footsteps ascending the stairs. He greeted me with his heart-warming smile and a peck on the cheek.

"How's it going? Looks like you've been busy."

I looked up while placing some notes in a file I had marked, "Bedroom," and kissed him back. "It's going great. I'm having a blast. This feels more like a designer job than construction, but there's a lot of stuff to build if Everleigh likes my ideas." I handed Slater a file. "Here, check it out. This is for the finished basement."

Slater took a seat next to me and for the next few minutes, he browsed over my notes. "These are great. I'm impressed." He flipped another page over and read some more. "I'm sure she's going to love it. I know her nephew will." He laughed. "What little boy wouldn't?"

I reached over and gave his knee a squeeze. "Thanks. What time is it?"

He glanced at his watch. "Almost six."

"Oh shoot. I got so involved in this stuff that I forgot about dinner."

"Don't worry about it. I planned on taking you out for dinner anyways."

I grinned. "You did? What's the occasion?"

He tapped the top of the files on the desk. "This. We are celebrating our new job. Now, come on. You've done enough for today."

I laughed and gave my hair a toss. "But we don't have the job yet. I don't want to jinx it."

"Oh, I think we got this one. Let's go, I want to take you to the seafood restaurant that just opened up."

"Cool." I stood and tried to skip out of the way of Slater, but I wasn't fast enough and he quickly slapped my backside as I brushed by him. "Give me a minute to grab a jacket," I said, on my way to the bedroom.

The restaurant was only ten minutes away and the parking lot was busy. Seemed we weren't the only ones trying out the new place in town tonight. Slater managed to squeeze his truck in between two other large trucks, with barely enough room to open the doors. Once he had it in park, I reached into my purse for my brush and gave my hair a quick comb. Slater looked at me with a loving gaze. "You don't need to do that. You're already gorgeous."

I leaned in and gave him a deep, passionate kiss, searching for his tongue with mine. "Thanks, babe. You're not so bad yourself." I giggled.

Turned on by the taste of his breath, I continued to kiss him, rolling my tongue against the roof of his mouth. For a second, I opened my eyes and looked out of Slater's window and was shocked to see a middle-aged man peering at us from the truck parked next to us. Sitting next to him was another man in the driver's seat, looking over his friend's shoulder, into our truck. Both were smiling.

I was turned on instantly and changed my kisses to short quick, feathery ones. "Don't turn around. Just keep kissing me," I whispered between breaths before giving him more pecks on the lips. "Two guys are watching us from the truck parked on your side."

I gave Slater a huge flirtatious smile, who smiled back and immediately pulled me in closer. "Well, damn, girl. Let's give them something to look at," he said before grabbing the back of my head and pulling my mouth to his. With force, he fed his fingers threw my hair and kissed me hard as I slid into his lap and faced him.

My back was pushed against the steering wheel, but I didn't care. The fire within had been ignited again and my body tingled with passion. I broke away from our kiss and leaned back against the wheel, pushing out my breasts, with now prominent nipples peeking through the thin white material of my t-shirt. Slater took a deep breath as he admired my breasts, just inches from his face. "Are you not wearing a bra?" he asked in a sexy, alluring voice.

I gave him a mischievous smile. "Oops, I guess I forgot to put one on."

"Lucky me," he whispered before dipping his head between my breasts. I gasped from his touch and held him close to my chest. "I want to taste them. Lift up your shirt."

I didn't object and as I hastily lifted my shirt, I glanced quickly at the men in the truck. They were still watching us, their eyes glued to the window. Their grins told me how much they were enjoying the view. As soon as my breasts were free, Slater grabbed them with both hands and pushed them together, I gasped again and threw back my head as he nibbled on my nipples and circled them with his warm tongue before taking them in his mouth simultaneously.

"Oh, Slater!" I squealed, while grinding my crotch against his prominent bulge. Rotating my hips against his jeans, I pick up speed as he continued to suck on my breasts and knead them deeply in the palms of his hands. Again, I tossed my hair back as I reached down and began caressing his now hard bulge with deep, sensual strokes as Slater released a loud moan. "Let's give them something to watch that will be imbedded in their minds for a long time," he said between moans. "I want you to go down on me."

I was beyond caring. "Oh my god, yes."

Wasting no time and with a racing heartbeat, I climbed out of Slater's lap and together, in haste, we undid his pants and pulled them down to his ankles, along with his boxer shorts. For just a moment, I admired his beautiful shaft, stroking it with my hand, before shadowing it with my lips and taking him deep into my mouth. With soft, gentle strokes, I used my tongue to caress and circle his crown. Slater settled back into the seat and released repetitive satisfactory moans as I worked him to an orgasm. It didn't take long, and once the last drop of semen fell against the roof of my mouth and he gave one final thrust, I felt his body relax as he stroked my hair and curled it around his finger. "Fuck, Sabela. You're amazing."

I giggled again and quickly wiped my mouth with the back on my hand, then raised my head out of his lap. I was facing the window and saw the two guys grinning and nudging each other. I smiled as they gave me two thumbs up. "Well, they seemed to have liked the show." I laughed while making room for Slater to pull up his pants. Slater turned to face them, smiled, and gave them a nod. "Are you ready to go eat?"

"I just did," I said sarcastically.

Slater smacked my thigh. "Well then. You can have dessert."

As I waited for Slater to finish dressing, the truck next to us fired up, and we both looked in its direction. The guy closest to us was wearing a huge grin and waved as the driver backed out and honked his horn. I giggled. "We certainly made their night."

Slater took my hand. "Feels good, doesn't it? No harm was

done. We were just sharing our pleasure." He gave me another passionate kiss. "Come on, beautiful. Let me buy you dinner. You've earned it." Before stepping out of the truck, he held my cheeks tenderly in his palms and looked at me lovingly. "I love you."

"I love you too," I said with a loving smile.

CHAPTER 8

Today was turning out to be a fantastic day and it wasn't over yet. First, there was the news Sabela had secured a great job that was going to make life much easier for a while and hopefully get us out of debt. The kitchen renovation was way ahead of schedule, thanks to Travis, and we should be able to wrap it up a day early, and then my girl just gave me head in front of two strangers in my truck. Damn, life was good.

We were both in terrific moods as we walked toward the entrance of the restaurant with a dance in our steps. As always, we felt liberated from our recent sexual adventure of being watched. Afterwards, we shared our little secret with each other with laughing eyes and endless giggles that left us with a childish sense of naughtiness. While still snickering and swinging each other's hand, we entered the crowded restaurant and was told there would be a fifteen-minute wait.

"Let me go freshen up," Sabela said as I quickly claimed the corner of a long bench that stretched the entire wall. There was just enough room for two people. I quickly took a seat and admired Sabela's behind as she skipped off to the restroom.

We ate at a small secluded booth and like every time we eat out, I sat next to Sabela, never across from her. There was something about feeling her body pressed up against mine that made the meal much more enjoyable. Fondling her thighs underneath the table while I ate with the other hand was all part of the meal and if she was wearing one of her sexy mini dresses, well, I could guarantee you my fingers would definitely begin to wander up to her beautiful crotch.

Feeling her thighs push against mine as she spread them to greet me in the secrecy of our booth was such a turn on. Especially when we were surrounded by a room full of strangers. It's tough to keep my cool and not molest every part of her body at that very moment but there have been a few instances where I managed to bring her to orgasm with the magic of my fingers.

But the consequences I must suffer were well worth it. I instantly knew when she was about to climax the minute she buried her head into my shoulder and clenched my skin through my clothes with her teeth, to drown the orgasmic cries she must desperately release. But tonight, Sabela was wearing jeans so both she and my shoulder would be safe.

Our meal was superb, and the service was the best I'd ever experienced. I think Sabela and I just found our new favorite restaurant. The view was spectacular, overlooking the Pacific Ocean, like many restaurants in the area. Content and full, Sabela rested her head on my shoulder as we cuddled in each other's arms and sipped on a glass of red wine. I figured now was a good time to bring up the wedding. "You know, this new job might finally allow us to plan our wedding."

Sabela raised her head, smiling. "Do you think so?"

"I think it's time. Don't you?" I kissed her forehead. "I want you to be my wife." I laughed. "And soon," I added with a tickle to her waist.

Sabela twisted her body to avoid my hand. "Oh, Slater. Every day, I think about becoming your wife." She took my hand and stroked the top of it delicately with two fingers. "We don't have to have a huge elaborate wedding that costs a ton of money. I want it to represent us and be within our means." I could see the excitement in her eyes as she paused for a moment. "I've given this some thought." She rolled her eyes. "Well, a lot of thought, actually. How does a beach wedding sound?"

"I love the idea. I was thinking the same thing."

Her eyes shone. "Really?" Enthusiastic to share her thoughts, she sat up straight and faced me, still clutching onto my hands. "I thought about the beach, because that's where we met, and of course you love to surf. How do you feel about a sunset wedding? We could make an arbor out of driftwood and I can drape some sort of sheer white material over it."

Listening to her ideas, I could picture it all in my mind. "It sounds perfect."

"We could have teepee lights all over the place, and white lilies —which are my favorite. We could find someone to serve us seafood and after we've taken our vows we can swim together in the ocean. Fully clothed!" she added with a laugh. The excitement could still be detected in her voice.

I pulled her in close, so our noses were touching, and kissed her with all the passion I was feeling. I felt the goose bumps rise on my skin and the pitter-patter of my heart as I spoke to her. This was what real love felt like. Without Sabela, I was nothing. "I think it's perfect. We're going to set a date soon, I promise. As soon as we know what this job is paying us, this will be the first thing we check off our list."

Sabela looked at me with misty eyes. "It's going to be a beautiful wedding. I can't wait to say, I do, *to you,*" she said before closing her eyes and kissing me softly again.

Reluctantly, I changed the subject. "When do you meet with Everleigh again?"

"I'm going to call her tomorrow and see if we can meet the day after. In fact, I wanted to talk to you about that. How is the kitchen renovation coming along? Do you need me tomorrow? I was really hoping I could stay home and get all of the plans I have organized, so that I'm ready when I meet her."

I shuffled in my seat. My butt was beginning to feel numb from sitting for a long time.

"With Travis's help, we're ahead of schedule. It will be fine if you stay home. I think it's a great idea. The sooner you present your ideas to Everleigh, the sooner we can get started." I paused and took a sip of wine. "This job will be finished in a day or so, and we have nothing else going. I'm having Travis help me tomorrow with the granite countertops, so we should be fine."

"Great! I'll get an early start and call her around lunchtime. Do you think you can get away for an hour when I see her? She's hasn't met you yet, and you *are* the other 'S' in S & S Construction, you know."

I laughed at her remark. "You're right. I do need to meet her. I'll make a point to get over there when you meet with her again."

"Thanks. Maybe you'll have some ideas too when you see the place."

"I can't wait to see it after what you've told me." Suddenly, I had a thought. "Hey, should I bring a change of clothes."

"That's a damn good idea. I hadn't thought about that. Her place is immaculate. Yeah, pack a fresh set of clothes and change before you come over."

I wasn't sure if it was a good time to bring up the email I had received from the couple. We hadn't talked about our wild fantasy in days with everything that was happening, and I wasn't sure if it was just a spur-of-the-moment fantasy when we were caught up in the moment, or if Sabela actually wanted to pursue it. I decided to mention it so I would know whether to reply or not.

"Hey, I got an email from one of those couples this afternoon." I waited anxiously for her reply, trying to read her expression. She looked stunned.

"Really?" She fell back into her seat. Her eyes drifted away from my direction. "Wow. I never thought anyone would answer."

I placed my hand on her arm. "What do you think? They gave me a phone number. They want me to call them."

She turned and gave me a devious smile, and I felt my tensed nerves relax. She was still okay with this crazy idea we had come up with. "Are you going to call?" she asked.

"Only if you're okay with it. I have no intentions of meeting these people. We just want to see how they operate."

"Can you imagine having sex with each other in a room while someone watches. I'm getting turned on just thinking about it." I saw the sparkle in her eyes as she played out the scenario in her head and had to chuckle.

"Well, should I call?" I asked, placing my hand on her knee.

"Yes! Call them. But I want to be there when you do. You can put it on speaker. Let's see what comes of it. We may never do anything after all, but I know we'll have hot sex as soon as we hang up the phone." She laughed.

"Sounds good to me. We'll do it this weekend, after we've wrapped up this job and secured a start date with Everleigh. In the meantime, let's go home. I want to fuck your brains out."

CHAPTER 9

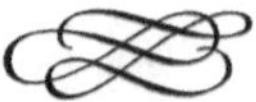

SABELA

The next morning, I couldn't wait to get started on the Everleigh project. I wanted to have everything perfect for her and woke up at six in a sweat, worrying about it. Unable to sleep anymore, I quietly rolled out of bed, making sure not to wake Slater. Thankfully, the sun was beginning to rise and I didn't need to turn on any lights. I grabbed my bathrobe that was draped over the closet door and tiptoed out of the room, closing the door quietly behind me. After making a pot of coffee and pouring myself a cup, I settled myself in the office and got started.

Around seven, I heard movement coming from our bedroom and then the shower running, letting me know Slater was awake. I knew if I popped into the bathroom to say a quick, "Good morning," I'd end up in the shower with him. It always happened that way. I just couldn't resist him, especially when I looked at his gorgeous naked body, drenched in trails of water and smeared with soapy lather. Nope, this morning I had to block out the images I was having of him at this very moment as I listened to the calling sounds of the shower. I must not give in to my temptations and stay focused on my work.

As hard as it was, I managed to remain in the office and felt somewhat relieved when I heard the water go silent. Twenty minutes later, a fully dressed Slater with damp hair popped his head through the doorway of the office. "What time did you get up? I didn't hear a thing."

I turned my head and gave him a smile. "Around six. I made a pot of coffee."

He entered the room and leaned over my chair to give me a kiss. His breath tasted fresh and minty. "I'm running late. Call me after you've talked to Everleigh," he said as he headed toward the door. "Love you!"

"Love you too. Bye!"

Once the house was silent, I returned to my task at hand and didn't move from my desk for the next six hours. I was so engrossed in my work, I lost track of time and never called Everleigh around noon like I wanted to. If Slater hadn't called me a few minutes ago to check in, I'd still wouldn't have known what time it was. I spent the next half hour finalizing everything and placing it orderly in the files before calling Everleigh. The phone rang a few times before she answered.

"This is Everleigh. Who's calling?"

I took a deep breath to calm my nerves. "Hi, Everleigh, this is Sabela, with S & S Construction. How is everything?" I asked using my best professional voice.

"Oh hi, Sabela. I'm good. How are those plans coming along? I'm anxious to get started so I can start bringing Scottie here again."

"That's why I'm calling. I have some ideas I would like to go over with you. If you like them, then we can do the paperwork and set a start date."

"Wonderful! When can you come over?"

"I was hoping sometime tomorrow."

"Tomorrow is good." She paused for a moment. "Will Slater be with you?"

"He will be busy in the morning, but plans on meeting me at your house a little later, if that's okay."

"That will be fine. How does eleven o'clock sound?"

"I think that will be perfect. Slater will be able to come over on his lunch."

After saying our goodbyes, I immediately hung up the phone and called Slater. He answered right away. "Hey babe, I just got off the phone with Everleigh. We're on for tomorrow at eleven. Can you meet me there?"

"Sure."

"Great. Tonight, we need to go over my plans together and come up with some sort of estimate. If she okays everything I'm proposing, we could make quite a bit money. I'm guessing around $75,000, after expenses." I couldn't help squealing. "Can you believe it?!"

"Seriously. Fuck!" Slater sounded shocked when I gave him the numbers. "Easy street, here we come," he yelled in a gloriously happy voice. "I gotta go, babe. I love you. I'll see you tonight."

"Love you too. Say hi to Travis."

Later that night, Slater went over my plans and loved every aspect of them. "You're really good at this stuff. Look what you've done. I'm impressed. We might have to branch out and make you our designer." He looked at some of my notes a second time. "This is incredible. I had no idea you knew how to do this stuff. Where did you get all these ideas from?"

I shrugged my shoulders as I sat next to him, my legs crossed on the couch. "It wasn't that hard. As soon as she told me what she wanted, ideas just began flooding my brain. I couldn't write them down fast enough. You really think she'll like it?" I asked, feeling a little unsure of myself.

"I don't see how she couldn't. All the pictures you've gathered off the internet really helps."

Slater really knew how to boost my confidence. After sharing the files with him, I felt much better and couldn't wait to get Everleigh's thoughts. He also agreed on my numbers and even mentioned there was a possibility that if the job went on longer than the anticipated three months, our earnings could be even higher. In an excited frenzy, I jumped off the couch and did a stupid happy dance while squealing, "Yes!" at the top of my lungs. Slater laughed, soon joining me in my dance before slowing it down to a soft romantic smooch.

The following morning, I was up before Slater again and already in the shower by the time he woke up. He didn't waste any time joining me with his morning stiffy, which I gladly welcomed, and together, we extended our shower as long as possible. Starting my mornings with him inside of me was far better than any cup of coffee.

Feeling perked up from our morning sex session and two cups of coffee, I was ready and confident about meeting with Everleigh. After Slater left, I spent some time looking for a professional wardrobe and decided on a comfortable floral summer dress, with a red belt accessory and matching red pumps. I spent another hour in the office finalizing everything and when I was certain there was nothing more I could do to improve it, I gathered my files and purse and headed out the door.

I arrived at Everleigh's promptly on time and again took a moment to scan the grand surroundings of the neighborhood before heading up the cobbled stone path to the front door. I still wasn't feeling comfortable about parking in her driveway.

After ringing the doorbell, I stood back and waited. In no time, Everleigh answered the door, looking absolutely stunning. I was taken back by her beauty. It was obvious she had put some effort into dressing this morning. Her makeup was applied perfectly, and she had used a slight tint of blush to accentuate her high, prominent cheek bones. Shades of browns contoured her eyes, along with thick full mascara and black eyeliner that was penciled perfectly, bringing out the beauty of them. The deep red lipstick she had chosen was perfect for her skin tone, and she wore an elegant flared red dress that complemented her blonde hair. The jewelry she was wearing, which I knew were real diamonds, glistened from the sun seeping in through the open door. I drooled over the pear-shaped earrings and the three-inch cuff bracelet, knowing they probably cost more than I make in a year.

From the corner of my eye, I detected more glistening and turned to look at her hand where it rested on the door handle, noticing the three diamond rings. Her appearance was quite a change from the last time I saw her, in a workout suit and no makeup. Today, she seemed overdressed. Maybe she had an important meeting after me, but it wasn't my concern. I was here to get her approval of my plans and sign on the dotted line.

"Sabela, so good to see you. I can't wait to see what you've come up with," she said while motioning me into the house.

After entering and again feeling underdressed, I rubbed my feet vigorously on the doormat and followed her through to the kitchen, where we sat at the counter. A pitcher of iced tea and two glasses were already in place.

"Will Slater still be joining us?" Everleigh asked, while pouring some of the beverages into the glasses.

"Yes, he should be here in about half an hour," I replied, while looking at my watch.

"Wonderful. Now, show me your plans."

Over the next forty-five minutes, I showed her the plans I had put my heart and soul into, explaining every detail, color and, nervously, the cost, but she was thrilled with everything and didn't question any of them or suggest any changes. She didn't even flinch a muscle when I mentioned how much everything would cost. As we were wrapping it up and I was wondering where Slater was, my phone dinged. I checked the message.

Hey babe. I'm running late. I should be there in about fifteen minutes.

When I glanced up, I noticed Everleigh was also trying to read the message, which I thought was odd. "Was that Slater?" she asked.

"Yes. He's running a little late. I'm sorry. He should be here soon."

She looked relieved to hear he was still coming. "No problem. I have no other plans today."

So, she doesn't have an important appointment after me. Then, why the hell is she dressed to the nines?

Everleigh interrupted me from my thoughts. "Would you like some more iced tea?"

"Sure."

While we waited for Slater, we spent the time going over more of the plans and had moved to the bedroom we were going to renovate for Scottie's room when we heard the ring of the doorbell. "That must be Slater. Do you want me to wait here while you let him in?"

In what seemed to be a nervous manner, Everleigh folded her arms in front of herself and replied with an uncomfortable tone, "Why don't you answer the door. He may not come in if I answer."

Not understanding what she meant, I shrugged my shoulders. "Okay," I said, and headed down the stairs.

I beamed a big smile when I came face-to-face with Slater. He looked gorgeous and very professional, wearing tanned denim pants, a crisp white dress shirt with the top two buttons undone, and a pair of loafers. "My, you look good enough to eat." I chuckled with a flirtatious smile.

Slater pulled me in, wrapping his arms around my waist. "Don't tempt me." Before letting me go, he gave my body a glance over. "I love your dress," he said with his melting smile.

After entering the house, he did exactly what I did and wiped his feet with force on the mat. "Wow! You weren't kidding about this place." He scanned the house. "This must have cost a mint. Where is the lady of the house anyway?" Slater asked, taking in all the richness of the entranceway.

"She's upstairs." I took his hand. "Come on, follow me."

When we reached the bedroom, Everleigh stood in the middle of the room with her back toward us. "Everleigh, Slater is here," I said in a soft voice, afraid I was disturbing her.

Slowly, she turned around and looked directly at Slater. The room suddenly became cold. Slater let go of my hand and let his fall loosely against his side. He stumbled on his footing and took a step back. I couldn't help noticing how considerably pale his face suddenly appeared. It was like he was seeing a ghost.

"Eve."

There was a sudden uncomfortable silence in the room. Fear swept over me when I realized who this woman was, but I needed confirmation from Slater. "Is this the Eve you couldn't talk about?" I asked, my voice trembling.

He turned to face me, his body limp. I met his gaze, my worried eyes misty, anticipating his answer. "Yes, it is," he said, his head hung low.

His words stung me. I didn't know where to look or what to say. I was numb. When I realized who Everleigh was, my entire body became chilled, and I instantly felt deceived by this woman who apparently went by the name Eve. Slater reached for my hand, but I quickly pulled back, clutching my hands in front of my torn heart. Tears began to trickle down my cheeks. Afraid of saying words I'd only regret later, and being in the same room with her choked me, I had to leave immediately

"I have to go. I need some fresh air." I couldn't look at either one of them and instead, looked at the floor." I'm going to leave you two alone so you can talk," was all I could manage to say before heading for the door. "I'll be outside."

"Wait, Sabela!" I heard Slater call, but I couldn't talk right now. I needed to be alone.

When I reached the freshness on the outside, it suddenly dawned on me I had left Slater with a woman of his past. A woman I knew nothing about. I didn't know their history or what happened between them. All I knew was Slater couldn't talk about her. He'd never spoken of her, except for that one time when he told me about his parents. I needed to get away and process what was happening. As I wandered down the street, my arms crossed over my chest for comfort, fear swept over me. *What had I done?* Images of them falling into each other's arms like long-lost lovers clouded my mind. *Was I about to lose Slater?*

I couldn't go back. I didn't want to go back and just kept walking, procrastinating what I thought was going to be my breakup with Slater. I didn't want to hear those words, that he was sorry but it was over. What would I do? Where would I go without him? I didn't know how long I walked for. I was oblivious to everything around me. I walked in a daze, my eyes drenched with tears, my body numb and my heart in my feet.

After some time, I realized I couldn't run away anymore. I needed to hear from Slater and I needed to know about Eve. What did she do that was so bad that he couldn't talk about it? Taking a deep breath, I tried to pull myself together. Wiping my eyes and holding my head high, I turned around and headed back to my truck where I would wait for Slater. Unsure of what I would find, there was no way I was going back in that house.

CHAPTER 10

SLATER

When I found myself unexpectedly face-to-face with Eve, it took all my strength to remain standing. If there was a chair behind me, I would have easily fallen into it, shocked and numb by seeing her standing before me. A face from the past I had tried so hard to forget. A woman I had loved deeply, who had left with me with no explanation and had taken a piece of my heart with her. *What was I supposed to say to her? Am I supposed to act like nothing has happened? Like she never did those things to me. I can't. I won't.*

She spoke with uncertainty, seeing the shock that crossed my face. "Hello, Ian."

She called me Ian. I couldn't remember the last time someone had called me that. I adopted Slater after she left me. Before Sabela left the room, she echoed my birth name in a whisper.

"Ian?" Fear saturated her voice.

I couldn't speak. I was in a trance. Was she really standing there before me? All the hurt she had caused me so many years ago was beginning to resurface again. I could feel the anger I had suppressed starting to surge. I wanted to leave the room, never to return, but I needed to know why she was here. Why, after all this time, had she come back into my life? I stumbled with my words, unsure what to say. "Eve. My god."

"I'm sorry, Ian. I don't want to cause any trouble for you and Sabela," Eve said, reaching for my hand.

"Don't touch me!" I yelled as I increased the space between us. "Why are you here? What do you want from me?" I didn't give her a chance to answer. "Isn't what you've already done to me enough?"

I was furious Sabela had left upset, and began pacing the room to control the anger I was feeling toward her. "You've obviously done well for yourself," I snarled, waving my arms around at the grand room. "With your fancy mansion and diamonds. If you think I'd be impressed by all this and come running back to you, you're mistaken. I love Sabela and I'm going to marry her."

Thoughts of Sabela, sitting outside alone, wondering what was going on between Eve and I, crushed me. I released a cocky laugh. "In fact, you know what, Eve? I owe you a big thank you. If you hadn't left me, I would never have met Sabela." I turned and gave her a sarcastic grin. "So, thank you."

Eve tried to approach me, her hands held tightly in front of her. "Ian, I know you hate me. You have every right to."

I stepped back. I wasn't going to deny she was still as beautiful as I remembered. "I don't hate you, Eve. I despise you," I gritted through my teeth. "I don't know what little scheme you have going on here, but I want no part of it." I turned my back on her and stared out the window at the ocean view for a moment. Thoughts cluttered my mind of deceit and confusion. I faced her again, my arms folded. "The only thing I want from you, is an explanation. Why you left me like you did? And another thing? How the hell did you find me?"

"I can't go into any details right now on why I left you, but it will all make sense soon, I promise. As far as finding you, it wasn't that difficult. I knew how close you and Drew were, and I figured you guys would still be in touch, so I called him. I didn't tell him who I was. I simply told him I was looking for someone that worked for him by the name of Ian. A friend of mine had recommended him and I would like to hire him. He knew right away I was talking about you, and brought me up to date about your new company and gave me a number. I guess Sabela handles all the job inquiry calls?"

"Yeah, she does. It's probably a good thing because I would have hung up on you. I for sure wouldn't have taken the job, when I found out it was you I'd be working for." I was finding it difficult to look at her without feeling fury. I allowed my eyes to wander at the expensive paintings hanging on the walls and the lush area rug beneath my feet.

"So, what happened, Eve? Did you leave me for some rich dude? Obviously, it didn't work out, but I see you benefited from the breakup."

"Yes, I was a fool. I left you for another man. I admit, his wealth did attract me."

I blasted my words at her. "You were never satisfied when I was with you. Always wanting more than I could give you. So, where did you meet him?"

"Online."

I threw my hands in the hair. "I knew it! Let me ask you something?"

"Okay," Eve replied in a somber voice.

"Did you marry the guy?"

Eve crossed her arms in front of her. "Yes, but not right away. After a year of dating, I convinced him to marry me, and that's when I realized what a mistake I had made. He was a player, never home and sleeping with lots of women. I filed for divorce, and we agreed on a settlement."

"A hefty one, I see." I looked around the room again. "You still haven't told me why you tracked me down, and why I must do this work for you."

"I'd rather not say right now. Soon, you will know. Trust me."

I let out a loud sinister laugh. "Trust you! You want me to trust *you*? For the past week, you have deceived my fiancée by not telling her who you really are." I shook my head in disgust. "Do you know how hard she has worked on this project of yours?" I pointed to the doorway. "And right now, she is probably in tears after realizing who you are, and is more than likely afraid that she's going to lose me."

Realizing how Sabela must be feeling, in defiance, I marched over to Eve until our faces were just inches apart. "Let me tell you something. If you think I'm going to come running back to you, you've got another thing coming. There's not a chance in hell I'd leave Sabela for you. In fact, I shouldn't even be here. I should be down there with her." In haste, I turned and headed toward the door. "This discussion is over."

"Ian! Wait! Wanting to hire you was not a lie. I do. I will pay you well, I will make your life comfortable. It's the least I can do for the pain I've caused you." She paused and narrowed her eyes. "I am no threat to you and Sabela. In fact, I'm envious of what you two have. I know what a lucky woman she is." She curled her lip and released a subtle laugh. "I'm not going to lie. I've had dreams that you took me back, and it had crossed my mind since I've returned, but I saw the way Sabela's eyes light up when she speaks of you and I knew I didn't stand a chance." She took in a deep breath. "I won't do anything to jeopardize what you have."

She glanced at her wardrobe. "In fact, I feel kind of silly dressed like this. I don't know what I was thinking. I guess you could call it my last hoorah," she said, followed by a sarcastic laugh. "I could never be with you—not just because of Sabela." She took a deep breath. "But it's important to me that you work for me."

I stood, motionless, in the middle of the room, my back toward her. She sounded sincere. But how could I work for a woman that betrayed me? I turned my head. "Why should anything of importance to you matter to me? You never gave me a second thought when you simply vanished out of my life."

"I'm sorry, Ian. I'm not seeking your forgiveness."

I interrupted her. "Good! Because it will never happen."

She ignored my proclamation. "I'll make it easy for you. I'll be gone before you get here and I won't return until after you leave. You will never have to see me. I'll be visiting with my nephew until the work is done."

I was silent.

"Please say yes," Eve begged.

"Nothing about this is easy, Eve. I'm not even sure if I want to work for you. If Sabela refuses, then I will back her up. Her happiness is what matters here."

"I understand," Eve replied, her head hung low.

I wanted to know more. God, there was a lot I wanted to know. But, for whatever reason, she wasn't telling me everything. Even though I felt I deserved some sort of explanation.

"So, tell me. Your sister had a kid and she's now sick. Is that right?" I said in a calmer voice.

I noticed her hesitation before answering. "Yes, Lorraine is sick. She has a four-year-old son named Scottie. I'm doing all of this for him. He needs happiness in his life, and I want to give it to him."

"Where's the father? And I'm sorry to hear about Lorraine. She was always nice to me."

"The father is not in the picture."

"I see. What is wrong with Lorraine?"

Again, Eve hesitated. "I'd rather not say. It's not good, and I'm not ready to talk about it."

"Why are you not telling me everything?"

"I'm sorry. I can't right now." Tears began to pool in her eyes. "Please, Ian. Say you'll work for me. It has to be you."

I shook my head while raising my hands in defeat. "I don't know, Eve. I'm going to talk with Sabela. I honestly don't know if I can. I'm going to go. I'll have Sabela call you with our answer." Without saying another word, I left her alone in the room, feeling anxious to hold Sabela.

Standing outside the front door, I breathed in heavily, filling my lungs to full capacity with the fresh air. It felt good. I raised my head slightly and closed my eyes for a moment, allowing the cool breeze to sweep across my face. I needed this minute to compose myself and allow the anger I was feeling toward Eve to subside before facing Sabela. *God, I hope she's okay. What was going through her mind when she left me alone in that room with Eve?*

Feeling my heart rate return to normal, I headed toward Sabela's truck parked on the street, anxious to console her, but it was empty. In a panic, I spun around in a full circle, my eyes scanning the entire neighborhood for a glimpse of her. But she was nowhere to be found.

"Sabela!" The sound echoed across the serene streets, and then it became silent again.

Where is she? I continued to search my surroundings, refusing to leave the truck, knowing she had to return. I didn't want to wander the neighborhood, in fear, she may come back while I was gone and leave in her truck. I had no choice but to remain here and wait for her.

I pulled down the tailgate and took a seat. I could see more from here than sitting in the cab. I tried calling her numerous times on the phone, but she didn't pick up, which worried me more. I left numerous frantic messages, telling her I was waiting for her. I texted her the same messages. None were replied to. I didn't know how many times I checked my watch, but I knew it was at least every few minutes during the next half hour. I texted Travis and told him I was running late, and to do whatever he could until I returned. There was no way I was leaving without talking to Sabela.

The jingle of keys in the quiet, rich neighborhood caught my attention and I saw Eve leaving her house. She had changed into a more comfortable and more fitting wardrobe, consisting of black pants and a flared red top. Gold-rimmed shades covered her eyes. I watched as she walked toward her white Lexus, but she paused when she looked over and saw me, and instead headed in my direction.

"Fuck!" I spat under my breath, while scanning the neighborhood to make sure Sabela wasn't in view.

"Where's Sabela?" she asked, standing a few feet away.

"I don't know." I turned my head. "Go away. I don't want her seeing me talking to you."

Hearing my harsh words, she stopped, afraid to come any closer. "Do you want me to talk to her?"

I gave her a harsh stare and sneered at her unbelievable suggestion. "No!" I said with force. "You've done enough. Just leave before she gets back. I have nothing more to say to you right now."

Surprisingly, she didn't contest my request and simply nodded, followed by, "Okay" before she turned around and headed to her car. I watched with relief as she backed out of her driveway. I refused to look at her and when she finally drove off down the street, I relaxed my tensed body.

Another twenty minutes passed before I spotted Sabela turning the corner and walking toward me. I lifted myself off the tailgate and began sprinting toward her, calling her name. "Sabela!"

As I drew closer to her, her body language told me she was upset. She walked slow, clutching her hands in front of her chest. Her eyes were hidden by her shades, but I had a feeling she had been crying. With caution, I approached her, standing in front of her, my arms held out, and she stopped in her tracks. "Sabela. Are you okay? I've been worried about you."

Slowly, she removed her shades, revealing her red sunken eyes. My suspicions had been right. She had been crying. It crushed my heart to see her this way. "I'll know in a minute if I'm okay." She paused. "Tell me. Are you going back to Eve?"

I took her in my arms and held her tight. Tears instantly began to stream down her face, drenching my shirt. "Oh, Sabela, sweetheart. No. No, that's never going to happen. I love you." I pulled her away for a second, crouched my knees slightly, and looked her directly in the eyes. "You have nothing to worry about. I love you so much." I pulled her back in close to my chest "Come here," I said before I kissed her passionately on the lips.

She cried heavily as she kissed me back with the same fervor. "I love you too," she said, between her sobs. "I was so scared. I had to go for a walk and clear my head. I thought I was losing you."

"Oh, baby. You're never going to lose me. I promise."

She continued to cry. "Why is she here? You can't tell me this is a coincidence. She tracked you down, Slater." She took a deep breath to control her panicked heavy breathing. "She's up to something. I know it! She never told me who she was, and today, she was dressed to impress, and it wasn't me she was trying to impress."

I held her trembling body tighter, trying to reassure her she had nothing to worry about. "Oh, baby. I don't know what she's doing here, but I won't allow her to come between us. You must know that. I love you and always will."

Reassured by my words, her tears began to subside. "Slater, I need to know what happened between you and Eve. Will you tell me?"

Sabela was right. She should know what happened. We were a thing of the past. I had no secrets with her. "Yes, I will." I reached for my phone in my back pocket. "I'm going to call Travis and tell him I'll be another hour. I'll just hustle when I get back. This is more important."

After calling Travis and okaying everything with him, I told Sabela I wanted to get away from Eve's house and to follow me to a restaurant.

Once back in our familiar neighborhood, I pulled into a Coco's and waited for Sabela to pull up alongside me. As soon as she did, I jumped out of my truck to meet her and wrapped my arm around her as we walked into the restaurant.

Sitting side-by-side in the booth like always, we talked over our cheeseburger lunch. I didn't hold anything back. I told Sabela everything while I ate with one hand and she held the other. She listened without saying a word, as I started from the beginning, when we met in high school. I told her about us living together and how much I had loved her. I went on to tell her how devastated I was when she left me with no warning. At that point, Sabela squeezed my hand, showing me her compassion. "And since that day, I've not seen or heard from her since. Not until today."

Sabela shook her long mane of dark hair in disbelief. I watched as it cascaded over her shoulders, admiring every inch of her. "I can't believe she left you like that. Did she say why? Today, when you saw her."

"I asked her, and she only said she left me for some rich guy who turned out to be a player. I honestly don't care, and I actually thanked her for leaving me because if she hadn't, I wouldn't have met you," I said, followed by a laugh and a quick smooch on Sabela's lips.

Sabela slapped my shoulder, her jaw dropped, "You didn't?"

"Yes, I did." I turned to face Sabela and took both her hands in mine. I held them up to my lips and kissed them gently. Sincerity laced my voice. "Look, Sabela, I have no idea why she came back. She's not telling me everything. For whatever reason, she says she can't. All's I know is she wants to do a bunch of stuff for her nephew, and insists that we do the work."

"But why you?" Sabela asked with a puzzled expression.

I shrugged my shoulders. "I have no idea. I've made it clear to her that my utmost importance is your happiness, and I wouldn't do anything to jeopardize that. I don't care how much she is willing to pay us."

Sabela fell back in the booth, scrunching her eyes. "Oh, but the money is so good. Why does it have to be her? I worked so hard on that project." She leaned back and tilted her head. "This really sucks. I finally thought we were going to be living it up for a while." Suddenly, she leaned forward and frowned. "Oh, and our wedding. I was so looking forward to start planning for it. Now, we're going to have to wait."

I pulled her in and kissed her as she tucked her head on my shoulder. "Babe, she still wants to hire us, even after what I said to her. I told her I didn't know if I could. I honestly can't stand to look at her, and she said she'd be willing to be gone all day while we worked there."

Sabela raised her head, showing another look of surprise. "She did?"

"Yes, she did, but I told her I wouldn't give her an answer until after I've spoken to you. The job is still ours if we want it." I paused and squeezed Sabela's hand. "I'd do it as long as I knew you're okay with it, and if Eve keeps her word and leaves us alone while we're there. If she doesn't, then I'm out of there," I said, throwing my body back against the booth.

Sabela pulled away and leaned back while placing her hands on the table. Deep in thought, she began drumming her fingers. "Oh man, I don't trust her. She's already deceived you once. And me, for that matter. She's not telling us everything, I can feel it. But fuck! The money is too good to pass up."

I took Sabela's hands again. "Look, let's not make a decision now. Let's get back to Travis. He's gonna need help from both of us, and we'll stew on it for the rest of the day. Only do this if you're okay with it."

Sabela nodded and gave me a loving smile. "Okay."

CHAPTER 11

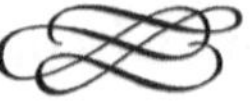

SABELA

For one terrifying moment, I knew how I would feel if I ever lost Slater. I never wanted to experience that feeling again. I was petrified. Listening to him talk about his relationship with Eve and putting everything in perspective put me at ease. When he spoke of her, he snarled her name, his eyes became sharp, and his fists would be clenched. I knew from his body language I had nothing to fear. It was Eve I feared, because she was obviously good at keeping secrets. She kept her online affair hidden from Slater for god knows how long. She began a friendship with me without revealing who she was, and she admitted there were things she couldn't tell us just yet, and I wondered why.

I didn't understand why she hunted down Slater to work for her. The only conclusion I could come up with, and what made any sense was that maybe she suddenly grew a guilty conscience about how she left Slater. Maybe this was her way of making it up to him. But I believed there was more to it than that. After hearing Slater's story, and her deception toward me, I knew I could never trust her and yet, I was considering working for the woman.

The only reason I was even considering it was because of the fucking money. *The root of all evil.* Slater and I had been struggling for so long, trying to catch a break or a big job that would finally put us over that hump, and money in the bank. This was supposed to be that job. Damn it. *Why did it have to be her?*

I agreed with Slater we shouldn't make any hasty decisions. Whatever she had up her sleeve, I wasn't going to allow it to ruin the relationship between Slater and me. We both must be on board with this and not allow her to jeopardize our relationship in any way. Slater and I must have each other's backs if we take this job.

When we got back to the job site, we found Travis leaning over the bottom cabinets in an

awkward position, trying to install one of the upper under-cabinet lights. He looked pleased to see

us. "So, how did it go?" he asked, straightening.

Slater and I looked at each other for confirmation on whether we should tell him what just went down. Slater shrugged his shoulders. "You wanna tell him?" he said with uncertainty.

A puzzled look appeared on Travis's face. "What happened?"

"Sure, I'll tell him," I said, replying to Slater. "I don't want to go into details, but to make a long story short, the woman that wants to hire us turned out to be Slater's ex."

"Oh fuck! Well, that makes things slightly uncomfortable," Travis said, shaking his head in surprise.

Slater joined in on the conversation. "Oh, that's not the half of it. I don't want to go into it right now, we've got too much work to do. How about we fill you in over a game of pool and some beers after work?"

I loved Slater's idea. The thought of chilling with some friends after the stresses of the day seemed appealing. "What a great idea!" I screeched before giving Travis a friendly slap on the shoulder. "You can call Jill and have her meet us. I've not seen her in a while and it would be good to catch up with her." I rolled my eyes and laughed. "Oh, she'd love this story too."

After I had mentioned Jill, I noticed Travis give Slater a sly look. I turned to look at Slater, but he quickly avoided eye contact with me. I sensed something was wrong. "What's the matter? Is Jill okay?" I asked with concern.

Travis didn't look at me either and instead looked down at the screwdriver he was twiddling in his hands. I approached him and placed my hand on his shoulder, tilting my head to see his eyes. "Travis? What's going on?"

He met my eyes. "Oh, nothing. Jill and I aren't getting along right now."

Upset by the news, I reached for my chest and gasped. "Oh, Travis, I'm so sorry." I turned to Slater, who was silent at the other end of the kitchen and leaning against the table with his arms folded. "And you knew about this?" I asked with a creased brow.

Slater's cheeks became flushed with guilt. He hung his head low. "Yeah he told me."

Travis butted in, sensing my unhappiness. "I asked him not to say anything. Don't be mad at Slater. I should never have told him in the first place. This is between me and Jill."

Travis's words put me at ease, and I realized Slater was put in an awkward position. I admired him for keeping his word to Travis.

"I'm sorry, Travis. If there's anything we can do, let us know, okay?" I gave him a friendly squeeze on his shoulder.

But Slater wasn't finished. His mannerism turned to frustration as he pushed himself away from the table and approached us. Standing between Travis and me, he turned to Travis. "I wish you hadn't told me. I don't like to keep secrets from Sabela. I just spent a good part of my afternoon telling her secrets I had kept from her about my ex. They always catch up to you in the end, man." Slater took a deep breath. "I think you should tell her the rest because if you don't, I will." Slater gave me a stare. "Now that she knows this much, I'm not taking her home until she hears the rest." Slater nudged Travis's arm. "Go on. Tell her."

Confused, I looked at Travis while he contemplated what to say, and then he just came out and said it. "I'm seeing someone else."

My jaw dropped. "What?" My first thought was Jill. "Does Jill know?"

Travis began playing with the screwdriver. "It's complicated," he said, without looking up.

"Of course it's fucking complicated!" I yelled, louder than I intended. "You're seeing someone else, and I'm assuming Jill doesn't know." He didn't answer right away. "Am I right?"

He finally looked up in my direction but continued to play with the screwdriver. "Not yet, but I plan on telling her soon."

I could feel the blood rushing to my head from the rage that was rising within me. I'd known Travis and Jill for many years, and never had I felt such anger towards him. I'd always thought they'd end up marrying someday, and now Travis had blown it. *How could he do this? And poor Jill.* I couldn't face Jill knowing this. "You have to tell her!" I insisted.

Noticing how quickly this had turned into a heated debate, Slater intervened. "Okay, guys, we're supposed to be working here," he said, stepping in closer. "Let's not let our personal lives interrupt our job at hand." He laughed at what he just said. "Ha! Who am I to talk. I just wasted half a day being pissed off at Eve."

I cringed when he said her name. "I know, Slater, but honestly he needs to tell Jill."

"Like I said, I will, real soon. If it makes you feel better, we've not been getting along for over six months now. I hate to say it, but it's been over for a while, Sabela. I told Slater the same thing," Travis said, using a solemn voice.

I appreciated Travis filling me in, but I was still saddened by the news. I gave Travis a friendly squeeze on his shoulder and softened my tone. "I'm sorry, I had no idea. I don't want to fall out with you over this." I let out a sigh, still upset by the news. "We all work so well together. We've been friends for a long time. But I do have to say this." Both Slater and Travis held their breaths, wondering what I was going to say next. "I can't see Jill until after you told her. I'll be avoiding her like the plague. So, tell her soon, okay? I miss her."

Travis nodded. "I will."

"Glad that's settled," Slater said with a huge sigh of relief and quickly changed the subject. "Are we still on for pool tonight?"

Both men looked in my direction, waiting for my answer. "Of course!" I said with a grin before opening a can of paint.

"Great!" both guys chirped before tackling the lighting together while I began painting the walls in the dining area.

That night, Travis's relationship woes were not brought up again. I didn't ask about his new girlfriend. I didn't want to know. I wasn't ready just yet. Instead, the three of us discussed the saga of Eve and filled Travis in on everything we knew.

Now that Slater had finally opened about his past with her, he explained to Travis with much more ease and acceptance. He was no longer haunted by the pain and deceit he had carried inside for so many years. He began looking at it as a blessing and while telling Travis how he was now thankful she'd left him because if she hadn't, he wouldn't have found me, he turned to look at me with his gorgeous, loving eyes and squeezed my hand.

It was at that moment, that Travis asked us a question. "So, what's stopping you from working for her?"

Slater and I were confused by his question and looked at each other with a puzzled look. To us, it was obvious. "She's my ex," Slater said.

Travis shrugged his shoulders. "So?"

Slater and I looked at each other again with blank stares, unsure how to answer. *Were we missing something?*

Travis could see we weren't understanding his logic or where this was going, and leaned in closer across the small round table, his elbows comfortably resting on the surface. "Look at you two. You're like two peas in a pod. You do everything together. What you two have is like super glue. There ain't nothing that's gonna tear you two apart."

Our frowns soon turned to smiles when we understood what Travis was saying was true.

"Jill and I never had that. It was all about the sex. As soon as that dried up, so did we. But you guys"—he leaned back in his chair and crossed his arms across his chest—"you've got the real thing going on. So, Eve is your ex." He raised his arms in the air. "Big fucking deal. Now's the chance for you to rub it in her face and show her how happy you are now."

We hadn't realized it right away, but Travis had made our decision for us. *What were we afraid of?* He was right, we had no reason to feel threatened by Eve. She might not be telling us everything, but whatever it was, we weren't going to allow it to affect us.

"You're right, Travis," I said triumphantly, while raising my glass in a toast. Our glasses dinged together followed by a chug of our chosen liquor.

Slater turned to me. "What do you say? Want to go work for the ex?"

I didn't hesitate with my answer. I was comfortable with my decision because Travis had made me look at it from a whole different perspective. "Yes. Let's do this!" I said, while giving Travis a smile and a nod. "Thank you, Travis, for letting me see how things really are."

He nodded. "Well, someone's gotta look out for you guys. You're so busy being in love, that you don't see the simple stuff."

I laughed at his accurate description.

Slater leaned back in his seat, looking serious. "Okay, so now that we've established that we will work for her, the big question is, who's going to call her?"

"I have no problem calling her," I quickly answered.

Slater couldn't hide his surprise. "Really?"

"Yes, really. This has been my project from the beginning. I'm not going to let her push me away and make me hide in some stupid corner, which is what she is probably hoping I would do." I shook my head and sat up straight. "I'll be fine. I have no problem calling her. Like I always say, we're in this together." I leaned in and gave Slater a passionate kiss on the lips. "I love you, babe."

"I love you too."

"And I love you both," Travis chirped in, disrupting our kiss. "I think we need another round of drinks," he added, flagging down the cocktail waitress.

"So, when do you want to call her?" Slater asked while Travis placed our drink order.

"Oh, in a couple of days. I want her to stew for a while." I sniggered.

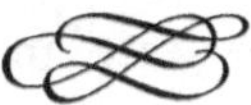

CHAPTER 12

I was shocked when Sabela said she would call Eve. She said it with such conviction in her voice that I noticed the change in her right away. Whatever intimidations she was feeling twenty minutes ago had completely disappeared. To her, this was a business deal, nothing more. It helped listening to Travis and how he saw the whole thing, and I think that's what opened her eyes. Mine too, for that matter. Sabela and I were a team and we did everything together. It made us stronger as a couple.

I wasn't sure how it was going to work out working for Eve but, like Sabela, I wasn't afraid anymore. I'd always have the original scars of hurt but I looked at what I had now and those days were a distant memory. Eve and I never had what I now have with Sabela. Looking back, I saw now that neither one of us were happy. She thought she'd be happier with someone else and I spent all my days, working my ass off trying to please her. We would never be friends. Like Sabela, I was approaching this as strictly business. We'd do our job, enjoy watching our bank account grow, and then get on with our lives. I had no intentions of staying in touch with her after the job was done. What she did was no concern of mine.

After confirming with Travis that he'd be at the job tomorrow, Sabela and I left the bar around eleven and drove both trucks home. As soon as we entered the condo, Sabela kicked off her shoes in the cute manner she always does—by kicking her heels high and pointing her toes high. I laughed as her shoes went flying across the room and thinking how lucky I was as I admired her trotting up the stairs. Halfway up, she stopped, twisted her waist so her butt stuck out in the provocative pose I knew so well, and looked over her shoulder at me. "I'm going to take a bath. Do you want to join me?" she asked with a leering smile.

Before I could answer, my phone chimed the sound of an email notification. "You bet," I said, pulling my phone out of my back pocket. "Go run the bath while I check this email. I'll be right there."

Before continuing up the stairs, she blew me a kiss. "Okay. Don't be too long."

"I'm right behind you." I chuckled, already feeling the rise in my pants, and hastily began checking my phone. My eyes grew wide when I saw it was from Susie and Vic—the live sex show couple. I read the message.

Hey guys! Just wanted to check in and see if you got our email. Can't wait to hear from you. Susie & Vic.

"Holy shit!" I said in a loud, surprised whisper while hearing the inviting water running from the bath upstairs. Skipping every other stair, I went up to tell Sabela, who was already standing naked in the bathroom, combing her hair. I stopped for a moment at the door and lusted over her beauty. She never failed to take my breath away. She looked at me through the mirror as she ran the brush through her long silky hair, which extended down her back.

My eyes wandered over her body, pausing at her perfect ass that was formed to perfection as she leaned over the sink to get closer to the mirror.

"Who was the email from?" she asked casually while inspecting her eye.

"You'll never guess." I smirked.

A frown appeared across her forehead. "Eve?"

That wasn't the answer I was expecting, and quickly told her before our night was ruined with a continued conversation of Eve. "No, Susie and Vic."

"Who?" Sabela replied, her expression blank.

"The couple off the internet." I jogged her memory as I approached her and wrapped my arms around her waist and gently kissed the crook of her neck

"Oh, shit! I'd forgotten about them." She gasped.

She turned to face me, locking her arms around my neck. I looked down at her naked breasts pressed against my chest and cupped my hand around one, massaging it gently as I spoke. "They asked if we'd gotten their email. They can't wait to hear from us," I said with a smile.

A slight blush tinted Sabela's cheeks. "So, are we going to email them back?" she asked before giving me butterfly kisses across my lips.

"I think we should discuss this in the bathtub," I replied as I broke away and began undressing, keeping my eyes locked on Sabela's.

Not breaking away from my stare, she walked over to the bath and descended her body provocatively into the bubbly water. The closing of her eyes and the huge relaxed sigh told me it felt good. I rushed to remove the rest of my clothes and stepped in behind her. Slowly, I eased my body into the comforting waters as Sabela moved forward to make room. With my legs on either side of her, I leaned back against the tub. Once I was comfortable, Sabela used my chest for a cushion. With her head resting on the left side of my chest, I reached over her shoulders and fondled her breasts as we talked. "So, do you want me to email Susie and Vic back?"

Sabela caressed my hands that covered her breasts. "That was the plan, wasn't it? To see how they set this stuff up. Before we advertise on our own."

I hesitated before I spoke. "Maybe we should see the whole thing in its entirety."

Sabela strained her neck to meet my eyes. "What do you mean?"

I smiled down at her. "I mean, maybe we should see how they do the whole show thing. You never know. It might be quite a turn on, watching a couple have sex. We'll see it from the other side. We'll be watching instead of being watched." I laughed.

Sabela rolled her body over in the water until she faced me. Her hands rested on my chest as she looked up. My attention drifted for a second when I noticed her butt cheek peeking out of the water, surrounded by bubbles. My hands itched to stroke them.

Sabela couldn't hide her surprise by my suggestion. "Really? You want to watch them have sex?"

Unsure if I had crossed our boundaries by mentioning the idea, I made sure to tread lightly. "I don't know. Just an idea that popped into my head. It might be kind of fun," I added with a subtle laugh.

Sabela stared at my chest while she drew circles on my skin with her finger, then looked up and gave me a seductive smile. "I bet it could be." She returned her focus to my chest and glided her tongue over my wet skin. "But not in the same room. That's too close for comfort for me."

She giggled as she worked her tongue over my chest a few more times, seducing me with every sensual lick. "Maybe we could watch from a distance on the beach. And they could watch us," she suggested as she pulled her torso out of the water and towered me. I leaned back further until my head rested on the rim of the bath, and took one of her breasts into my mouth, covering it completely as I reached around and took a firm hold of her butt cheeks and squeezed them hard. Sabela arched her back while releasing a loud moan. "What do you say?" she said between panted breaths. "Do you want to ask them to meet us on the beach?"

The fantasy consumed me as I continued to devour her breast and lightly tease her nipple with my tongue. "That would be cool," I whispered, as I blew my hot breath over her now erect nipple. Sabela gasped from the heated sensation. I squeezed her butt harder, pulling her in closer to my aching hard-on. "We could watch them while they watch us."

My words struck a chord of excitement in Sabela. She moaned a long drawn out, "Yes," before grinding her hips across mine.

I met her rhythmic moves, thrusting my hips towards her, allowing the water to splash over the sides and onto the tiled floor. "From afar, they would see me devour you, caressing your sunbaked skin smothered in suntan oil," I whispered into her ear as I reached beneath the bath water and placed the tip of my erection between her legs. With ease, she mounted me and took me completely as she released a long satisfactory moan.

"God! You feel good," she murmured while gyrating her hips. "I'd want to watch him take her just like you're taking me right now." Sabela kissed me forcefully on the lips and placed her hands on the rim of the tub behind me for balance. Arching her back, she tossed her head and rode me hard. With my hands on her hips, I quickened my pace while playing out our fantasy in a heated breath.

"Imagine, them watching us while we're watching them. God, what a fucking turn on that would be," I said, riding her harder and with more force. Wanting me to penetrate her deeper, Sabela arched her back even further, and her long hair cascaded behind her, dipping into the soapy water. Yearning to touch her tightened smooth skin, I reached up and massaged it deeply with the palm of my hand. Spreading my fingers wide, I explored her entire upper torso with deep circular strokes. She moaned from my touch. "I'd want them to see you come."

"Yes!" Sabela screeched with her eyes closed. "I know you would make me come good," she panted before her body became tense and exploded into convulsions of an electrifying orgasmic bliss.

I continued to thrust deep inside of her at great speed, knowing I was on the brink of a powerful orgasm. With one final push, I released a loud moan as I retuned my hands to her hips and climaxed amidst the splashing water. "Oh man, this feels so fucking good!" I yelled while feeling the glory of my juices spill inside of her.

After a few more thrusts, Sabela crouched over me, her hair dangling in my face. Our eyes met as we savored a long, drawn-out kiss, waiting for our heart rates to return to normal. Breaking the kiss, she lowered her body into my arms and laid her head on my chest and giggled. "We're bad."

I kissed the top of her head, enjoying the softness of her skin on mine. I drew her in closer, cupping her body with my arms. "You're a bad influence, girl. I just mentioned the email and within a few minutes, we're fucking like animals. What does that tell you?"

Sabela held her index finger up under her chin, like a thinker. "Hmm, that the thought of watching another couple turns us on?"

"I think you're right." I laughed and then did a reality check. "But we don't want to pay for it. Do we?"

Now that the fantasy had expired, Sabela agreed. "No. That's crazy. But I love when we fantasize because the sex is amazing," she said, followed by a sexy grin.

"Okay, that's settled. Glad we're on the same page. Who knows, maybe someday we'll find a couple to watch at the beach. The anticipation will be exciting though. I'm going to shoot them an email in the morning and tell them we've changed our mind."

Sabela looked up and gave me a pleasing smile. "Sounds good to me. We don't need to pay for it. We have our fantasies and a beach close by, which has never been a disappointment." She chuckled before spinning her body around, and rose to her feet. "Come on, let's go to bed. The water's getting cold. I'll clean up this mess in the morning."

Wanting nothing more than to curl up next to her, I followed her out of the tub and grabbed us both a towel from the rack.

CHAPTER 13

SABELA

After continuing our conversation in bed, the following morning, we sat down together and wrote Susie and Vic an email. We felt bad wasting their time, but we had no intentions of paying to watch people have sex. The money took away the fun of it all. For us, it had always happened in the moment and unexpectedly. The spontaneity made it thrilling. What if we weren't in the mood on the day we were supposed to meet them? Then what would we do? Force ourselves into the moment? No, that wouldn't work for us. We liked what we were doing now and decided to toss the idea of putting an ad in the paper too.

We wanted to be upfront and honest with them, and together we read what we had written before hitting the send button. With my chin propped on Slater's shoulder, I read the words on the screen.

Hi guys,

Thanks for getting back to us. We have to be honest and tell you, we've never done this before and were quite surprised when you responded. After a long discussion, we've decided to pass on the idea of meeting up with you.

We're sorry for wasting your time, but as much as we like to be watched having sex on the beach, this is an entirely different ballgame that we are uncomfortable with. I hope you understand and the best to the both of you.

Slater & Sabela.

I gave Slater a satisfactory smile. "I like it."

"Great," Slater replied before hitting the send button.

Even though we needed to get ready for work, I wanted a few more minutes with Slater after the email was sent. I leaned in and snuggled my head against his chest as I took hold of his hand and stroked it with my fingertips.

"You know, I'm glad we're not meeting them. I like our little episodes together, just you and me, with a few strangers looking on. I don't want to force anything that has to be arranged. It doesn't seem real that way. Does that make sense?" I asked. "Or am I just blabbering," I added, followed by a playful laugh.

Slater tightened his grip around my hand. "It makes perfect sense. Maybe someday, a couple will watch us on the beach." He scooched in his seat while adjusting his bulge through his sweats. "But you know something. If we continue with this conversation, I'm going to have to have my way with you. I'm already getting hard." He laughed. "Come on, let's go get dressed. I told Travis we'd meet him at eight."

I pulled myself away from the comfort of his body and rose to my feet. "Okay, party pooper," I joked, then added in a luring voice. "I guess we'll have to finish this talk tonight."

❧

At work, I wasn't planning on bringing up the subject about Travis's troubled relationship. But when I received a text from Jill, asking if I could meet her for lunch this week, I had no choice.

Travis was busy with Slater, prepping the floor for the slate tile that would be laid after lunch, and I was screwing in doorknobs on the cabinets when I heard the *ding* on my phone.

"Oh crap," I groaned after reading the message from Jill, then turned and looked at Travis. "Have you told Jill that you want to break up with her yet?"

Travis was kneeling on the floor and looked up in my direction. "No, not yet. I told you I would tell her soon. I just need to find a good time."

"I don't think there will ever be a good time, Travis," I said with a hint of sarcasm. "Christ! You're breaking up with her." I shook my head. "Well anyway, I just got a text from her, asking me to meet her for lunch. What am I supposed to tell her? I can't see her, knowing this shit about you." I rolled my eyes in disgust. "I've never turned down a lunch date with her. If I say no, she's going know something's up. Damn it, Travis!"

He laughed.

"Why are you laughing? This isn't funny."

He shook his head as he continued to snicker. "Wouldn't it be ironic if she wanted to meet you, so she could tell you that she wants to break up with me?"

I thought about his crazy notion for a moment but soon blew it off. "Why would she tell me first? Nah, I don't think so."

"Well, Travis told me first," Slater butted in.

I quickly saw I was losing this argument and waved my hands in defeat. "That's not the point. The point is, Travis needs to tell her. I'm going to text her and tell her I can see her next week." I pointed my finger at Travis. "That gives you a week to tell her. If you haven't by then, I swear I will tell her myself. I like both you guys and hate to see this happen. I'm sorry it didn't work out, but seriously, Travis? Jill deserves better than this."

"Yeah, I know, you're right," Travis agreed, before turning away and focusing on scraping linoleum chunks off the floor.

To add to the disturbing texts of the day, about an hour later, just before lunch, I got another one. This time, it was from Eve.

The guys were almost finished with prepping the floor and I didn't want to disturb them. We were on a tight deadline, so I left them alone and took a seat on the step of the front porch to read her message.

Dear Sabela, I'm truly sorry for misleading you and not telling you who I was. I realize now I should have been upfront with you from the beginning, but I was afraid if you knew who I was, you would never come to my house. Please forgive me. I know this is an awkward situation and I will do my best not to cause any more trouble for you and Slater. I see what the two of you have is very special and I promise I will not come between you. I hope you will still work for me. Like I've said, I will pay you well and will be gone when you are here so you won't have to see me. I'm sorry I upset you and Slater yesterday, and will do my best not to let that happen again. When the job is done, this will all make sense. That's all I can say for now. Please call me and give me your answer. Eve.

I reread her message a few times, letting every word sink in. Her text sounded sincere but after what she did to Slater, I just couldn't trust her. Our decision to work for her was made last night, thanks to Travis. She just didn't know it yet, and what did she mean by, "After the job is done, this will all make sense." What will make sense? *She* wasn't making any sense. I shook my head, puzzled by the comment, and headed back into the house, where I found the guys rooting through their lunchboxes.

"Hey, check this out. It's from Eve," I said, as I handed my phone to Slater.

A look of worry blanketed his face. "Oh crap. Is it bad?"

I folded my arms and leaned against the counter. "You tell me."

I waited while Slater, and then Travis, read her message.

Travis spoke first. "Well, sounds like she's sorry. Just do your thing. Make a bunch of money and move on."

I liked how Travis made it all seem so simple.

Slater read it again. "I've never known Eve to apologize for anything. Maybe this nephew of hers has changed her." He glanced over at Travis. "But I like your way of thinking, man."

Travis took a handful of chips before answering and held them in his hand while he spoke. "You have no ties to her. Just make sure she gives you a down payment before you begin the job, and have her pay you weekly, in case she tries to pull a fast one, like she did when she left you."

This time, I butted in. "Oh, I already plan on having some kind of payment plan set up when I talk to her. We need to have money coming in while we're doing the job. I'll make sure everything is in black and white. I'll write something up tonight, and nothing's going to happen unless she signs it."

"When do you plan on going over there?" Slater asked.

"Tomorrow. I'm going to text her back after I've eaten my lunch."

"Want me to go with you?" Slater asked with uncertainty in his voice.

I took another bite of my sandwich. "No. It will be less drama if you're not there. Besides, you guys have to finish this job by tomorrow." I looked around the newly remodeled kitchen. It was looking good. "Think you'll make it?"

Slater looked at their progress. "Yeah, we're right on schedule," he said with a pleasing smile.

After a short lunch break, the guys got back to work laying the slate tile, while I stepped outside to shoot Eve a text. It took a few attempts to get the wording right. I wanted to make it clear to her that her text didn't mean all was forgiven and I was now her new best friend, because trust me, that would never happen. Before hitting send, I read it one more time.

Eve, I don't want to discuss how I was totally left in the dark about the relationship you had with Slater. Your apology is accepted. Let's leave it at that. We are willing to have a strictly business relationship with you, and will do the job we had proposed, but only if our terms are met. I would like to meet with you tomorrow morning at 10:00am to go over them with you. Please let me know if that time is convenient. Sabela.

Satisfied with my text, I headed back into the house to finish up accessorizing the cabinets, but only made it to the end of the hall before my phone dinged. It was Eve telling me she would be expecting me at the time I specified.

"Okay, that's taken care of," I told the guys, sliding my phone into the back pocket of my jeans. "I'm meeting her in the morning."

Slater looked up from where he was kneeling, holding a tile. "Can't wait to hear how that goes," he said with a hint of sarcasm before putting the tile in place and pressing it firmly with his hands.

woke up the next morning with an edge to my attitude. I wasn't going to allow Eve to intimidate me. Keeping this on a business level, I dressed for the occasion, in black slacks and a dark green shirt. Not being my normal playful self and walked around the condo with a half-smile, Slater soon picked up on my demeanor and approached me where I was sitting on the couch, putting on my shoes. He sat next to me and placed his hand on my arm, stopping me from buckling my black sandal. "Hey, are you okay? Are you sure you want to do this?"

With my body still leaned over and my hand resting on my shoe, I looked his way.

"Yeah, I'm fine. Just warming up to the serious mode in preparation of talking to Eve. "I've got to prep myself," I said with a subtle giggle, which I could tell put Slater at ease. "I don't like the woman, but I sure do like the money part. It's the only reason I'm doing this." I finished buckling my shoes and gave Slater a friendly slap on the knee before rising from the couch. "Come on, you've got to go, and I need to go over the papers one more time before I show them to her."

I arrived at Eve's right on time; this time, not feeling belittled by her neighborhood. I didn't care how much money she had. The values I had as a human being were far superior than hers, I kept reminding myself, as I walked towards her front door, carrying a folder under my arm. It opened before I had a chance to knock and there she stood before me, but looking very different.

She was wearing no makeup. Her skin was extremely pale and her blonde hair, uncombed, hung limp over her shoulders. She wore black sweats and a matching sweatshirt. Her feet were bare. *Maybe she dressed this way for pity.* I didn't acknowledge her appearance or asked if she was okay because that would mean I cared, and I didn't.

"Hello, Eve. May I come in?" I asked.

She opened the door wider. "Sure, come on in. Can I get you some iced tea?"

I headed to the bar in the kitchen and set down the file. "No, I can't stay long. I just need to go over these conditions with you and set a start date for the project." I took a seat and slid the folder across the counter to her. She sat across from me and opened the file.

"As you can see, we will require a deposit before we begin working and funds for supplies," I said stiffly, as she read. "We request that you pay us weekly, and all business-related questions will be discussed with me. We think the suggestion you had of being away while we are here is a good one, but we will need a key." I let her read the rest of the contract in silence and waited with my arms folded for her response.

"You've thought of everything. Haven't you," Eve said, not shifting her eyes from the paper.

"I've tried to be completely thorough." I glanced over to see how much more she had to read. "I don't think I've missed anything," I added, returning to my space.

When she was finished, she slid the papers across the counter to me. I looked over at her, my brow creased. "Aren't you going to sign it?"

She didn't answer. Instead, she stood and proceeded to walk around to the other side of the counter. I watched, unsure of her next move. Before opening one of the drawers, she stared at me and gave me a subtle smirk but continued to remain silent. I avoided her intimidating stare and shifted my eyes to the papers for just a second before looking at her again. "I asked if you were going to sign them?"

She opened one of the drawers and pulled out a pack of cigarettes and a lighter.

"I didn't know you smoked."

She took one out of the pack, held it up to her mouth, and lit it, then took a long, drawn-out drag before talking. "There's a lot you don't know about me," she said behind an invasive plume of smoke.

I turned my head to avoid a collision with the vial stench that was traveling my way, but it was too late; I was surrounded by a cloud of smoke. I raised my hand and coughed hard as my eyes began to water.

"I'm sorry. Is the smoke bothering you?" Eve asked, before taking another hit and walking over to one of the patio doors. "Here, I'll open a door."

I coughed again and wiped the moisture off my cheeks. "Thanks. I've never smoked and it tends to hit me pretty hard."

Eve stood by the open door to finish her cigarette. "I don't smoke much, but the way my life's been going lately, I've been enjoying them a lot more."

I stayed at my seat, my hand resting on the papers. *I couldn't leave until she had signed them.* I tried one more time. "Eve, I really need you to sign these." I patted them with my hand and watched her take another hit, happy to see the smoke swirl out through the open door.

She turned my way. "Don't you think we should talk?"

I shifted on my stool, not wanting to get into this. I just wanted her to sign the damn papers so I could leave.

"I don't think there's any more to say." I uncrossed my legs and crossed them again. "You agreed, I covered everything."

Eve shook her head in disagreement—the cigarette had given her confidence. "Oh, come on, Sabela. You know what I mean."

I did, but was trying really hard not to go there and didn't want Eve to go down that path either.

"I'm not sure what you mean?" I patted the papers once more. "I went over everything with you and if you'd simply sign them, I can begin making plans for us to start."

"That's not what I meant and you know it." She took the last drag off her cigarette and stubbed it out in a plant pot by the door before closing it behind her. The smell of smoke lingered in the room as she returned to her seat at the counter. "I know we've started off on the wrong foot, but I'd like to start over."

I hate to admit it, but she was sounding sincere and the subtle friendly smile she gave me seemed genuine. "Start over in what way?" I asked.

She straightened her back before resting her elbow on the counter. "I like you, Sabela, and I'd like us to be friends." Her eyes drifted to the floor in pity. "I don't have many friends. In fact, I don't have any," she corrected herself with a slight chuckle.

I refused to feel sorry for her and wasn't going to allow her to get under my skin—what she did was unforgivable as far as I was concerned. "I'm sorry, but I don't think that is possible. I would like to keep this strictly business." I reached for the papers and picked them up. "We appreciate this opportunity, and we will do a damn good job, but I can't give you any more. I'm sorry," I said, handing her the papers.

She didn't hide her disappointment. "I'm sorry you feel that way," she said while browsing over the file in her hand, then she looked my way. "Maybe we can at least try on improving our relationship." She paused. "Is that an option?"

"It's always an option. I'm just not sure if it's possible under the circumstances. I just wished you had been honest with me from the beginning." I hesitated, feeling the need to defend myself and my reasoning. "I'm sorry, but I just don't trust you." The words sounded harsh and for a moment, I regretted saying them, but I knew they had to be said.

Eve simply nodded and didn't try defending herself. "I understand." She gave me what seemed to be another genuine friendly smile and said, "Well, I can only hope," then released a heavy sigh. "Things would be so much better if we were all friends."

I ignored her last comment. "Can I have you sign the papers now?" I glanced at my watch. "I really must get going."

She stood and walked toward the kitchen. "Sure, let me find a pen."

I quickly pull one out of my purse and held it up. "I have one."

Eve took it and returned to her seat, and pulled the papers in front of her. "Where do I sign?"

Eagerly, I point with my finger. "Right here." I told her and then held my breath.

But she didn't sign right away. Instead, she put the pen to her mouth and pondered a thought. She looks over to me, her eyes narrowed. "You know, I'm trusting you with my house and allowing you to be here alone." She tapped the pen on her lips. "Can't you trust me a little bit?"

I was not in the mood for a debate and folded my arms while wearing a slight frown. "I've given you no reason not to trust me." My patience was wearing thin and I began drumming my fingers on the counter. "I've been completely honest with you from the start." I paused, unfolded my arms, and sharpened my tone. "And I have nothing to hide."

I wondered if I was being a little too harsh to a woman who was hiring me and paying me well. But I couldn't help myself—I had to be honest and put all my cards on the table before we began the job. It was important to me she knew upfront where we stood. I refused to pretend, even if a big paycheck was at stake. I couldn't work under those conditions. For whatever reason, it was important to her we do this work, even though I made it quite clear I didn't like her, yet she still insisted on hiring us.

Eve didn't try to defend herself and nodded in agreement. "Well, I can't argue with that," she replied, pulling the papers in front of her and giving them a glance. "Okay, where do I sign again?"

I leaned in closer and pointed one more time. "Right here."

With bated breath, I watch her sign the papers.

"Here you go," she says as she slid them over to me and handed me back my pen.

"Thank you." I nodded while scanning over the documents. "Everything looks good. We just need to figure out the finances." Talking about money made me uncomfortable. Maybe it's because $50,000 was a lot of money. I'd never handled that amount of cash at one time. This was going to be the first payment toward supplies and labor for the first week.

Eve took a sip of her iced tea and rubbed her eyes. I noticed she suddenly looked tired, but I didn't acknowledge her fatigue. "How about I give you a credit card for the rest of the expenses after this week, and just give you a check for labor each week?"

"Sure, that would work," I agreed.

"Great." Satisfied, she slapped the surface of the counter with the palm of her hand, then quickly rose to her feet. "I'll have one set up by the end of the week."

I gathered up the file, making sure I had all the papers, and stood as well. Eve was already in the kitchen, lighting another cigarette.

"Well, I think we're all done here. I just need a check from you," I asked, turning my head away from the incoming cloud of smoke.

I tried to hold back a cough but failed, resulting in a hoarser cough than if I had just coughed naturally.

She held up her cigarette between two fingers, "Boy, these really bother you, don't they?"

I nodded amid my coughing attack. "Mind if I wait on the deck for the payment?' I asked, while rubbing my now watery eyes. "My eyes are burning."

"Sure, go ahead." She took another hit. "I'll be right back with a check. Who do I make it out to?"

With my hand on the door handle, I turned to face her. "S&S Construction," I replied, before stepping outside onto the large spacious deck and filling my lungs with fresh air. I welcomed the solitude of the space outside and allowed myself to free my mind of the hateful thoughts I had towards Eve. It wasn't going to be easy working for her, but I was pretty good at biting my tongue when I needed to. I had a feeling I'd be doing that a lot here.

I breathed in some more of the glorious air and filled my lungs to capacity—*damn, it felt good.* I glanced in through the glass doors to see if Eve had returned. She hadn't, so I decided to walk over to the other side of the deck and check out the view. It was amazing and I wasn't going to lie—I envied Eve having this right outside her door. From where I stood, I could hear and see the ocean below, crashing against the shore. Other expensive homes surrounded by tall elegant palm trees and well-manicured lawns shared the same view. The breeze that combed through my hair was refreshing. I closed my eyes and held my face up to the skies. One could not help but think life was good while standing here.

My tranquil moment was interrupted by a tap on the glass door. I turned my head to see Eve looking out, holding up the check. I nodded and scurried back inside. She was already in the kitchen, standing with her back toward me, pouring herself another glass of iced tea. "The check is on the counter," she said, while returning the pitcher to the stainless-steel fridge.

I approached the counter and picked it up. A grin escaped me as I looked at all the zeros, and I felt my hand tremble for just a moment. Never had I held this much money in my hand before—it felt fucking awesome. I opened the file.

"Thank you. Let me give you a receipt." I pulled out the receipt book and tucked the check inside, making sure it was secure. Eve stood in silence, sipping on her tea, while she waited. I handed it to her and closed my file.

She opened a drawer in the kitchen and pulled out a key, dangling on a sunflower keychain., and held it out to me. "Here is a key to the front door."

I took it. "Thank you."

"Let me know when you plan on being here, and I'll make sure I'm not here."

I nodded, my expression remaining serious. "I will." I placed the file under my arm. "I'll talk to Slater and get back to you in the next few days. I'll order the first round of supplies ahead of time and have them delivered here before we start."

Eve took another sip of her tea. "That will be fine, I'll have them put them in the garage. There's not much in there."

Relived this awkward meeting was finally coming to a close, I picked up my purse, shifted the file securely under my arm, and extended my hand. "Okay then. I think we're done here."

Eve looked at my hand, hesitating for a moment before taking it. Her shake was fragile and weak, and the cold temperature radiating off her skin stunned me. "I'll show you out," she said before setting down her glass and heading toward the front door.

Once I was seated in my truck, I had the urge to look at the check again. I pulled it out of the file, and giggled the moment I had it front of me. I still couldn't believe it.

"Fuck!" I yelled out loud. "I need to call Slater."

CHAPTER 15

SLATER

It was hard for me to concentrate at work this morning, wondering how Sabela was doing with Eve. I wish she hadn't been so stubborn, and let me go with her. But I learned early in our relationship, when Sabela's mind was made up, you just accepted it and went with it.

She finally called when Travis and I were eating lunch at a nearby Subway. Travis threw me a grin before I answered the phone. "I hope it's good news," he said between bites of his ham sandwich.

"Yeah, me too," I replied before picking up my phone. "Hey, babe. How did it go?"

I held my breath, waiting for her answer.

"Baby, we are on easy street!" Her voice was ecstatic. I could feel the huge smile as she spoke.

I let my tensed nerves relax for the first time since I said goodbye to her this morning. "You're fucking kidding?"

"Nope, I'm not kidding. I'm looking at a $50,000 check right now," she said before breaking into a loud, joyful laugh. "Can you fucking believe it?"

I was stunned and I scrambled with my words, but nothing was coming out.

"Baby, are you there?" Sabela asked, puzzled by my silence.

I shook my head in disbelief. "Yeah, yeah, I'm here. Fuck. Fifty thousand fucking dollars." I looked over at Travis, who nodded and raised his hand for a high five, which I immediately gave with a super-sized grin.

"So, how was she? Did she give you a hard time?" I was dying to know.

Sabela composed herself after her outburst of giggles. "Well, she asked if we could be friends, and I told her there wasn't a chance."

"You're kidding, after the crap she pulled. What did she say when you told her no?"

"What could she say? I let her know exactly how I felt and for whatever reasons, she insists on hiring us. But I've got to tell you."

"What?" I asked, expecting some bad news.

"She looked awful. She had no makeup on, and was wearing some old sweats and no shoes. It's none of my business how she dresses, but it was such a drastic change from the other times I've seen her."

I chuckled at Sabela's observations. I guess women pay more attention when it comes to one's wardrobe. Me, on the other hand, I didn't think it was such a big deal. "Well, maybe that's how she dresses when she lounges around the house all day. I wouldn't think too much about it."

Sabela defended herself. "Oh, but you didn't see her. Trust me. I'm not exaggerating when I said she looks awful." She paused for a moment and quickly changed her tone. "Anyway, enough of Eve. I want to go to the bank and deposit this check. Do you need me over there?"

"No, Travis and I have everything under control. We should be able to wrap it up by the end of the day. Do what you have to do, and I'll see you tonight at home."

"Oh, fantastic. After I've gone to the bank, I can spend the rest of the day figuring out what to order for Eve's job." She said sounding relived. "Oh, and tell Travis I'm seeing Jill in a few days, so he'd better tell her soon what's going on."

"I'll tell him," I said, glancing over at Travis.

Travis looked up. "Tell me what?"

I whispered to Travis while Sabela was still talking. "Jill."

Travis rolled his eyes and went back to eating his sandwich. "Okay, babe, you can tell me the rest tonight. I love you."

"I love you too, baby." She screamed into the phone, "Fifty thousand dollars! I can't fucking believe it," before hanging up.

"Shit, that's awesome, man," Travis said, sliding his plate to the side.

"Yeah, no kidding." I took a sip of my Pepsi. "Looks like I'll be able to keep you employed for the next few months."

Travis leaned back in his seat and belched a couple of times while enjoying the aftermath of a good lunch. "Thanks, man. I really appreciate it."

I shook my head in protest. "You don't have to thank me. Shit, you'd do the same for me and besides, I really need you on this job. It looks like Sabela is the designer for this one." I chuckled and took another sip of my Pepsi, then chose my next words carefully while playing with the straw in my drink. "But you know, you should tell Jill soon what's going on."

I paused to see Travis's reaction. Looking down in his lap, his arms now folded, he kept his gaze down and simply nodded.

"You gotta tell her before Sabela sees her." I continued to stare at Travis, hoping for some sort of response, but he remained silent. Feeling irritated, I sharpened my tone. "Hey, I'd appreciate it if you don't leave it up to Sabela to do your dirty work."

Travis picked up on my harsh tone and looked my way. "No, no. Of course, not." He shifted in his seat and began tapping his fingers in a nervous manner on the table. "I wouldn't do that. I plan on telling her tonight. I think it's best I move out this weekend anyway." He combed his fingers through his hair and leaned back again.

"Probably best, given the circumstances," I said in a softer tone. I could tell this wasn't easy for him and I didn't want to make it any harder.

"Yeah, we got into a big fight last night." This time, he pulled his hair back away from his face. "I should have told her then and just got it over with, but she was going on about stupid crap—picking fault with everything I do."

I could tell Travis needed to unload his frustrations, so I remained quiet and just listened, nodding when it seemed appropriate.

As he spoke, his skin became tight and his lips narrowed, expressing the anger he had kept locked up inside.

"If I'm gonna be honest, the reason why I said nothing was because I was hoping she would tell me first that she wanted to break up. After all the shit she said about me, I don't even know why she's still with me." He slammed his fist on the table. For a second, the restaurant fell silent from the loud sound. "Damn it! Why didn't I tell her?" he said, and then let out a harsh laugh before glancing my way. "If I had, we wouldn't be having this conversation."

"True." I picked up my drink and empty plate as I nodded. "Well, it sounds like neither one of you want to be together, so stop living in misery and tell her tonight, like you said." I glanced at my watch and stood. "In the meantime, we've got a job to finish."

Travis grabbed his plate and headed to the trash can. "Yeah. Come on, man. Enough of my problems. Tell Sabela not to worry."

I threw my plate in the trash after Travis. "Thanks. She'll be happy to hear that."

Travis and I were able to finish the job by the end of the day And I must say, we did a damn good job. Mike came home just as we were packing up our tools. He had nothing but praise for us and thanked us for making his wife happy. After handing me the check, he gave me a firm handshake. "Thank so much, Slater. When we get around to remodeling the bathroom, I'll be calling you."

"Sounds good." I picked up the last of my tools and headed out the front door. "Enjoy your night," I yelled over my shoulder, and after putting the drill I was carrying in the back of my truck, I walked over to Travis's truck, which was parked behind me.

Travis was on the phone, but quickly hung up when I approached the window. "You didn't have to hang up, I would have waited," I said.

"Nah it's fine. I don't want to keep you waiting. What's up?"

"I just wanted to say thank you for your help. If you want to follow me home, I'll have Sabela write you check."

Before Travis could answer, his phone rang. "Damn it!" he said, and quickly glanced at the screen.

"Do you need to take that?" I asked.

"Nah. She can wait. I told her I'd call her right back." He chuckled. "Women. They have no patience."

"Is it Jill? You can give me a call whenever you want to come over. I'm heading straight home."

"No. It's the woman I've been seeing," he said, leaning his head back against the seat.

A thought just occurred to me and I was hesitant about asking Travis. But from what I was seeing, his problems weren't only at home with Jill. "Hey, can I ask you something?"

"Sure."

"Does the woman you're seeing know about Jill?"

He let out a sarcastic laugh and drew out his words. "Oh yeah, she knows. She's getting on my case about ending it with Jill too."

He sharpened his tone. "In fact, she threatening to dump me if I don't tell her soon."

I could tell the mess Travis had gotten himself into was beginning to take its toll. His eyes told me he cared about his new girlfriend but also saw the fear when he mentioned telling Jill.

"Look man, I don't want to get in your business, but you can't keep going on like this. Do what you said earlier. Just go home and tell Jill." Reaching in through the window, I gave him a pat on the shoulder. "Call me tomorrow. I'll have a check ready for you."

Travis didn't budge. I could tell his mind was going crazy. "Sure. Say hi to Sabela."

"Hey, when things calm down, why don't you bring your new girlfriend over for dinner. We'd love to meet her," I said in a more upbeat tone, trying to perk up Travis's mood. Then I realized something. "What's her name anyway?"

I couldn't help noticing how uncomfortable my question made Travis. Shifting in his seat, he grabbed the steering with both hands and stared down at his phone in his lap. "Oh, that's not important right now. Let me get through this and then I'll have you meet her."

"Wait. Do we know her?" I asked, noticing his sudden nervousness.

He hesitated before answering. "Let's not get into this right now. I've got enough to worry about." He fired up his truck. "I'll call you over the weekend."

I had a strong suspicion we knew Travis's girlfriend, but I wasn't going to pressure him into telling me. Like he said, he had enough to deal with right now. But I couldn't help tossing names through my head on who it might be, only to come up empty. When Travis put the truck in gear, I stepped away. "Okay man. Well, good luck."

He glanced up and grinned, but it was fake. "I'm going to fucking need it," he said as he pulled away from the curb.

On my drive home, I kept thinking about who Travis might be

dating. When I asked if we knew her, I saw the sudden terror on his face. He was definitely afraid to tell me. Who the hell could it be? And did Sabela know her? Then I realized, of course she knew her—Sabela and I share the same friends. This was beginning to not look good. For whatever reason, Travis was not ready to tell me the girl's name. Why was that? It seems there was more to this than what he was telling me. I gave up. Maybe when I told Sabela, she'd have an idea who it might be.

Two blocks from home, my phone dinged with a new email. I told myself to remember to check it when I got home.

When I walked through the front door, I was welcomed by the delicious aroma of baked chicken coming from the oven. I followed the scent, breathing in heavy, and saw the dining room table was set for two, along with candles and flowers. Sabela didn't cook too often, but when she did, I knew I was in for a treat because she was one hell of a cook.

"Hey, babe! I'm home," I called from the bottom of the stairs, assuming she was in the office.

"Be right there," she hollered back.

"Something smells really good down here," I said, taking off my shoes at the table, then remembered I needed to check my email. I pulled my phone out of my back pocket and looked at the screen. "Holy fuck!" It was from Susie and Vic. I leaned back in my chair, stunned. "I wasn't expecting to hear from them again," I mumbled to myself.

Before I could read the email, I was distracted by Sabela walking down the stairs, wearing the sexiest black mini dress and matching heels. Leaving my phone on the table, I stood to greet her at the bottom of the stairs. She looked stunning—I would never get tired of looking at her.

When she reached the bottom, I noticed the sexy black choker with a single black rose in the center, circling her neck. I took her hand and pulled her in close. "Wow! You look gorgeous," I said with a luring smile. "I love your outfit." Turned on by her presence,

I devoured her lips with mine. "Damn, woman. I can't get enough of you," I confessed after reluctantly pulling away.

Hanging her arms loosely around my neck, my arms locked around her waist, she rubbed her nose with mine and whispered in my ear, "Tonight, it's just you and me, babe."

"Hmm, I like the sound of that," I whispered in response and kissed her again.

"We're going to celebrate life on easy street with some good food and music." She swayed her hips from side to side, rubbing her crotch across my groin. "Soft music, candlelight, and a home-cooked meal. How does that sound?"

Moving my hips in sync with hers, I reached behind and pulled up her little black dress and grinned. "No panties."

She puckered her lips and pressed her finger against them. "Oops," she replied in a cute sexy voice. She broke free of my hold and led me to the kitchen by the hand. "Come on, I want to show you what I've cooked. Have a seat."

I fell into the chair she pulled out for me, wondering what I ever did to deserve her. Admiring the view, I watched while Sabela bent at the waist in front of the oven. *She knows what she's doing.* As if she could read my mind, she looked over her shoulder and wriggled her ass just enough to get my juices flowing, and blew me a kiss.

"Keep this up and we're skipping dinner," I told her, adjusting my now hard cock.

She giggled before opening the oven door, and waved the aroma blasting from the oven in my direction. "Hmm, that smells so good. Ready to eat?" she asked.

Unable to take any more of her teasing, I stood and approached her from behind, wrapping my arms around her. "If we don't eat within the next five minutes, I swear I'm going to do you on the dining room table," I told her before kissing her ravenously on the neck.

"Okay, okay!" she squealed in laughter before twirling out of my arms and over to the counter to grab the oven mitts. Together, we flirted, we kissed, and we danced around the kitchen while we brought the meal to the table. Once everything was in place, Sabela softened the lights, lit the candles, and played some soft music on the CD player. It was the perfect romantic night for two people who were crazy in love with each other.

After our meal, our eyes strained from gazing at each other, Sabela lifted her glass of white wine and leaned over the table, her elbow resting on the surface. "You know, we can plan our wedding now."

I leaned over to meet her and took a sip of my wine. "Yes, we can."

"Still want a beach wedding?" she asked before finishing her wine.

I smiled through my words. "Yes. I can't think of anything better."

The memory of our first encounter reminded me of the email from Susie and Vic. I was so distracted by Sabela I never read it. I picked up my phone that had been pushed to the side.

Sabela's brow creased. "You're going to check your phone in the middle of our romantic dinner?"

I laughed. "Now hold on a second. You might like this," I told her while opening the email app.

Folding her arms, she spoke in a humorous tone. "Well, it better be damn good. I plan on having sex with you soon."

"Oh, that's gonna happen...trust me." I opened the email and gave her a devious grin. "We got an email from Vic and Susie today."

Sabela's jaw dropped as she unfolded her arms and fell back in her seat. "You're kidding. What did they say?"

"I have no idea. I was so captivated by you that I haven't had a chance to read it."

Sabela was up out of her seat and leaning over my shoulder before I had the email opened. "I want to see what they said."

Together, we read the text on the screen.

Hey Guys,

Thanks for getting back to us and we totally understand. Don't feel bad. Believe me, I chickened out a few times in the beginning when we decide to do this stuff. But hey, we like the fact that you liked to be watched at the beach. So do we . We go to Black's nude beach every Sunday from sunup to sundown. Look for the giant blue and smiley umbrella. You can't miss it. Maybe we can watch each other sometime?

Vic & Susie

After reading the text, Sabela took the phone out of my hand and read it again. "Where the hell is Black's Beach?" she asked, still looking at the screen.

I shrugged my shoulders. "I have no idea."

She was still standing and I turned in my seat to face her. She saw the opportunity, handed me my phone, and took a seat on my lap, dangling her arm around my neck. "I didn't know San Diego had nude beaches," she said with a devilish grin.

I caressed her back through the lace material of her dress, our mouths within inches of touching. I brushed her hair away from her face with my other hand. "Imagine the fun we could have there."

Sabela licked her lips. "I'm getting wet just thinking about it."

Sliding my hand up under her dress, I pulled her in for a kiss. The kiss was long and drawn out. Our tongues circled, our eyes were closed. My hand explored the soft skin of her thigh – tracing the defined muscle tones with delicate strokes. "We should check out the beach sometime." I kissed her again, brushing my tongue over her lips. "What do you say?"

She returned the kiss, but harder, pushing me back in the chair, and her hair tickled my face. "I love the idea of lying on the beach next to you, naked." Her hand moved down to my now prominent bulge and she squeezed it hard.

I moaned. "I think we need to go to bed and discuss this."

She gave my cock another firm squeeze before pulling herself off my lap and standing. Keeping her eyes focused on me, her moves were slow and seductive. "I think we have a lot to talk about," she whispered, taking my hand and pulling me to my feet.

Her warm breath blanketed my face. I took a deep breath and slipped my hand up under her dress to pinch the cheeks of her naked ass. She ground her hips and circled her ass over my hand. "I want you," she murmured before kissing me.

Pulling away, I took her hand. "Lead the way, pretty lady. I can't wait to peel that dress off you." I smirked. "But the choker stays."

CHAPTER 16

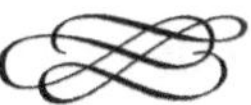

SABELA

*S*ex was at its finest last night. Turned on by our endless fantasies, we became uncaged and wild. We were ravenous and had no boundaries. We fucked hard and when we thought we were done, we did it again. Driven by a desire to explore the nude beach and the possibilities that may occur, we knew we would be taking Vic and Susie up on their offer from afar someday. We had no intentions of introducing ourselves, but we had full intentions of watching them and hoping they'd watch us.

This morning, I couldn't help smiling. I felt liberated and completely satisfied, and yes, a little sore. But it was a good sore. Now, it's 7:00 a.m. Slater was still sleeping, and I was surprised I was up so early, considering I had my last orgasm around 3:00. But I was so excited about life at the moment I just couldn't sleep. I kept trying to wrap my head around the fact that for the next few months, we would be making ten thousand dollars a week. That was forty thousand dollars a month and I couldn't fucking believe it. I needed someone to pinch me, to tell me this wasn't a dream.

For the next few months, we'd push through this job, no matter how weird or difficult it got and then we could finally start planning our wedding. I couldn't wait.

The first thing I planned on doing after my coffee and shower was to text Eve and let her know we planned on being there Monday morning at nine. *I hope she can be out of the house by then.* I then needed to text Jill to see if we could meet for lunch over the weekend because I wouldn't know when I'd have any free time after that. *Travis better have told her about his affair by then. And how will Jill be if we meet?*

Slater finally faced the morning a few hours later and beamed at me as he walked down the stairs, looking as fine as ever, wearing a pair of faded jeans and no shirt. "Hi, beautiful," he said, followed by a yawn and a comb of his hair with his fingers. "What did you do to me last night?" he asked after another yawn.

Already showered and dressed, I placed my laptop on the coffee table and stood up from the couch where I had been working. "Hi, babe. Looks like you had a rough night." I smirked. "Want some coffee?"

"Yeah give me a gallon." He laughed and took a seat at the kitchen table.

"Here you go," I said, and placed a fresh cup in front of him, before joining him.

For the next few minutes, I watched and admired him while he savored the hot liquid. Even half asleep with mangled hair, he tickled my heart. *God, I love him.*

"Damn, that tastes good," he said between sips. "Geez, I feel like I have a hangover, but I didn't get drunk last night." He gave me a cheesy grin. "Oh wait. I was drunk on you," then laughed out loud at his corny joke. "Isn't that a song."

I nodded. "Yep. Luke Bryan sings it." I changed the conversation to work. "So, I texted Eve and told her we could start Monday. She got back to me and said that's fine. Are you good with that?"

"Yep," Slater said, followed by another drawn-out yawn.

Over the next few hours, we discussed the job and went over

the plans. Slater needed to take a bunch of measurements for the basement remodel and the play area outside before ordering materials, and said he would do it first thing Monday morning with Travis.

"Do you think we will be able to finish all of this in a few months? "I asked, feeling a little concerned.

"I was wondering the same thing. I thought about giving Drew a call and seeing if I could hire a couple of his guys for a while." He glanced at the plans for the basement. "That's going to take some work."

I pumped up from his suggestion. "I think that's a great idea. Can you call him over the weekend?" I asked, eager to get this thing going.

"Yeah, I'll call him later today. Oh, and I almost forgot, Travis may stop by for his check today."

"Oh good, I need to talk to him." I leaned back in my chair. "I might be having lunch with Jill this weekend. I'm waiting to hear from her. Do you know if he's talked to her?"

Slater chuckled. "It's funny you should ask. I was going to tell you last night, but we got distracted and I forgot."

I was all ears. "Go on."

"Well, he did say he was going to tell her last night, but when I asked who this other woman was, he didn't want to tell me. He actually looked afraid when I asked." Slater stared at me with a serious look. "I've got a feeling we may know her."

My jaw dropped and I raised my voice, startled by his suspicion. "You're kidding!"

"Well, I'm not certain, but he definitely avoided my question, and I could tell he couldn't wait to leave. He left me wondering who the hell it could be, but I can't think of anyone." He paused. "Do you have any idea?"

Folding my arms, I thought for a minute. "We don't know that many people. When I got fired, I didn't keep in touch with most of the girls." I laughed sarcastically. "I was too busy getting to know you. Most of the women I know I are in relationships."

I had a funny thought. "Oh shit, what if the supposed woman is having an affair too?" I leaned back and chuckled. "Shit, this is like a goddamn soap opera." I thought some more and shook my head. "I have no idea. Maybe it's someone we both know at the local market or something. Or a girl from dental school—but I lost contact with them a long time ago. The only ones I see are Jill and Cathy, and I've not seen her in a few months."

I stood and poured my cold coffee down the sink. "I guess we'll have to wait and see," I said, turning to face him and ushering him out of his seat. "Now come on, finish getting dressed. I want to go spend some of Eve's money on decorations and paint for the bathroom. I can work on that while you guys do the heavy work."

Slater raised his hands in defeat. "Okay. Okay," he said, before downing a large gulp of coffee and heading up stairs.

Left alone at the table, I turned to my phone for entertainment, but was soon interrupted by a text message. It was from Jill.

Hey girl, can we do lunch this afternoon? Would love to see you. Get this, I'm single again. Tell you more when I see you. Hugs xoxo

After reading her message, I couldn't help releasing a huge sigh of relief. Travis had broken up with her, but it was sad to read. The four of us had some good times together, and I realized now those days were behind us. I read her text again and wondered if Travis had told her he was seeing someone else. She didn't say anything in her text. I glanced at my watch and texted her back, letting her know I could meet her at two and suggested a restaurant we visited often—Tico's Taco's. A few minutes later, she replied with a thumbs up emoji.

I didn't know why but when two o'clock rolled around, I found I was super nervous to meet Jill. I didn't know if I should ask about the other woman—what if she didn't know? Then I'd really be putting my foot in my mouth, and probably make things a lot worse than they already were. And what if she asks...do I lie? I'd never lied to Jill; I didn't know if I could. God, this sucked. Why did they have to break up?

When I pulled into the parking lot, I immediately spotted Jill's car. Only because it stood out like a sore thumb—she's the only person I knew who drove a pink Mustang. I remembered when she took it in for its paint job a couple of years ago. Everyone at work knew her favorite color was pink and when she told us she was getting her car painted pink, we all thought she was joking. Nope, she wasn't. It's the brightest pink I'd ever seen.

I parked a few cars down from her, checked my face and hair in the rearview mirror, and grabbed my purse before stepping out of my truck. Once inside the restaurant, I scanned the dining area and saw her toward the back, sipping on a bottle of beer. She didn't see me, and I made my way to her table.

I slid into the seat across from her and couldn't help noticing how awful she looked. Normally, she wore her chestnut-colored hair in a ponytail, and I didn't think I'd ever seen her without earrings, but today she wasn't wearing any. Her hair wasn't tied back either; it just hung loosely around her face, with no shape or body. Makeup was absent too. Without it, her eyes seemed much smaller and her cheekbones were nonexistent. She wore no lipstick, and her lips seemed to just blend in with the rest of her face.

"Hey," I said, unable to hide the pity in my voice. My heart ached when I saw how lost she looked.

She quickly glanced up. "Hey." Then, she continued looking at her bottle of beer with a blank stare, which she was holding with both hands while resting her arms on the table.

"Are you okay?" I asked, reaching out and touching her hand.

She pulled away and took a swig of beer before leaning back in her booth. "Fucking Travis broke up with me," she snarled with hatred in her eyes.

"I'm so sorry."

Jill took another drink, but it was a gulp not a sip this time. "I knew we weren't getting along but fuck, man, he doesn't even try and work it out." She shook her head in disgust. "Three fucking years I've wasted with that guy."

I listened, not knowing what to say. Both Travis and Jill were good friends. I didn't know why their relationship went south, but it tore me up, knowing it couldn't be saved. "Did Travis move out already?" I asked, waving down a waiter.

"He's moving his shit out now as we speak. I didn't want to be there, which is why I texted you," she told me while finishing off her beer. "I told him to leave the key on the counter. I don't want to see him."

The waiter approached our table. "Want another beer?" I asked. She nodded and I ordered two. "Where's Travis moving to, do you know?"

Jill didn't look up and continued to stare at her empty bottle. "Probably with his new fucking girlfriend." She finally looked my way again. "I didn't tell you that part, did I."

So Travis did *tell her.* "No, you didn't. Any idea who it is?" I knew I was prying here—I was dying to know who he was dating.

"Fuck no! And I don't want to know." She scanned the restaurant. "Where the fuck is our beer?" she griped.

"It will be here soon," I said, trying to calm her down. I couldn't blame her for being angry. Travis should have ended their relationship before hooking up with someone else. He said it was over months ago, and Jill just said that too. But it didn't matter—being dumped for another woman had to sting, even if you no longer cared about the person dumping you. Jill wasn't upset, nor was she shedding any tears. All I saw was rage.

"Did you suspect he was seeing someone?" I asked, and instantly regretted it, thinking it may be too soon to ask such questions.

Finally, the waiter arrived and placed two bottles of beer in front us. "Can I get you anything else?"

Jill was busy taking a large gulp, so I answered. "No, thank you. We're good."

He nodded and left the table.

"Hell no, I didn't know he was cheating on me," she snapped. "Do you think I'd stay with him if I did?"

Embarrassed by my stupid question, I shied away from her glare. "I'm sorry, that was dumb of me to ask."

Jill continued to vent, her face muscles tight as she spoke. "I can handle the breakup part—shit, I saw it coming. But fuck, why did he have to hook up with someone else first, and then tell me it's over." For a minute, she was quiet, contemplating her thoughts. "I don't know why it bothers me so much. I don't love him anymore, I haven't in months, and I'll be fine. It's just shitty what he did." She looked at me for validation. "Don't you think?"

I squirmed in my seat—I didn't want to be in the middle of this breakup and have it ruin the friendships Slater and I had with Jill and Travis. I chose my words carefully, trying to make sense of Travis's actions that I didn't entirely agree with.

"Yes, it's shitty what he did. He should have been honest with you or, like you said, broken up with you months ago. But neither one of you took the plunge to end your relationship, even though you both knew it was over." Contemplating Jill's reaction, I took a swig of my beer before saying any more. "Maybe he didn't know how to end it, just like you didn't. But now that he's met this other woman, he had no choice."

Jill nodded, her tone softer. "Yeah, but it still sucks."

I took her hand, and this time, she didn't pull away. "I know it does, hon, and I'm not trying to make excuses for what Travis did, or take his side. I'm just trying to understand it." I gave her a warm smile. "I love both you guys, and I'm sorry this happened, but I think you're going to be okay. You said yourself you don't love Travis anymore."

Jill let go of my hand and gave her hair a good toss. Composing herself, she sat up straight and spoke with a sharp tone. "You're right. I'll be fine. I just needed to vent. Are you hungry?" she asked, picking up the menu.

Seeing Jill pull herself together, I smiled. "I am. Let's order some food. It's on me."

Jill finally smiled—subtle, but it was still a smile. "Thanks."

I wasn't sure if it was the third beer Jill ordered with lunch or the large portions of tacos that she ate, but by the time we were through eating, her mood had definitely changed for the better. She relaxed her hunched shoulders, spoke in a softer tone, and even saw the funny side of her breakup by cracking a few jokes.

"It would have been better if I was the one that went out and found somebody else first." She laughed before leaning over the table and grinning deviously. "Hey, do you know any sexy, single guys?"

"Jill! You haven't been single for twenty-four hours yet."

Her tone turned cocky. "Well, Travis didn't even wait until he was single." She laughed.

Raising my glass and feeling lightheaded from my third beer, I agreed. "You've got a point." Remembering what Slater had told me about finding extra help, I told Jill. "Hey, Slater is thinking about hiring some extra help for the new job we're starting this week. Maybe one of them will be cute and single?" I grinned before taking another sip of my beer.

Jill picked up another taco and spoke between bites. "Yeah, Travis told me about it. Says you guys will be making some money."

I was surprised she knew. "Travis told you? I thought you guys weren't getting along?"

"I guess you could say we tolerated each other. There was never any big fight or anything…we just grew apart. He did his thing—which, obviously, was fucking another woman—and I did mine."

I stopped her for minute. "You have cheese on the corner of your mouth," I told her while wiping it off with my finger. "There you go."

Jill picked up a napkin and wiped her mouth. "Thanks. Where was I?" Remembering, she gave her head a quick shake. "Oh yeah. Travis and I were still on speaking terms. We were more like roommates, I guess. Anyway, he told me he'd been working with Slater last week, and then went on to tell me that Slater wants him to work for the next few months at new job you're starting next week." She stopped and gave me a serious look. "Hey, is it true?"

I gave her a puzzled look. "Is what true?"

"That you'll be working for Slater's ex?"

"Oh, Travis told you that too, eh? Yeah, it's true. I don't want to get into it right now. I'm fine with it."

Jill's eyes lit up. "Wow! Well, I heard she'd be paying you well. No wonder you took the job." She chuckled. "I wouldn't care who the fuck it is…I would too."

I leaned back and folded my arms. "Yeah, the money will be good. We can finally think about planning our wedding."

Jill squealed. "Yeah! You'll have to have me help you plan it." In a matter of seconds, her jaw dropped and her eyes became wide. "Oh shit!"

"What?" I asked, confused by her sudden mood change.

"Will you be inviting Travis to the wedding?"

"Well, yeah." And then it hit me. "Oh shit."

I shook my head, not wanting this to become an issue right now. Jill was feeling better and I wanted to keep her spirits up. "Let's not worry about that now. The wedding is months away. A lot could happen in that time. You and Travis may be friends by then."

"I honestly doubt it. But hopefully, I'll have a date to bring," she said, followed by a snarky grin.

"Hey, are you going to be able to afford your place on your own?" I asked.

After taking the last bite of her taco, Jill leaned back in the booth and folded her arms. "I'll probably have to get a roommate. In fact, at work, a new girl, Sadie, started last week and she mentioned she wants to move out of her mother's place. Maybe I'll ask her. She seems nice."

"That's a great idea. Better ask her soon before she finds a place. How is the rest of the gang anyways?"

Jill took a sip of her beer. "Yeah, I'll ask her Monday. Everyone is all still there. Even your favorite, Claire," she said with sarcasm.

I shook my head in disgust before taking a swig of my beer. "Oh god, don't get me started. Does she ever mention Davin?"

"Nope, and we never ask," Jill replied, shaking her head.

"Well, that's good to know." I glanced at my watch. "Hey, I really have to go. You gonna be okay?" I asked, reaching for her hand.

"Yeah, I'll be fine. Thanks for listening."

"Hey, that's what friends are for. You don't have to thank me, silly."

I flagged down the waiter and asked for our check.

Jill checked the time on her phone, "I should get going too. Travis should be gone by now."

After I signed the lunch check, Jill picked up her pink jeweled cell phone off the table and together, we walked out to the parking lot, where I gave her a tight hug. "Now, you call me if you need anything, okay?"

Jill nodded. "I will. I love you, girlfriend."

"I love you too," I said, walking away, again wondering again who Travis was dating and how he and Jill were going to be at our wedding.

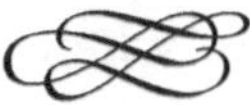

few hours after Sabela had left to meet Jill, Travis showed up at our house while I was watching the football game. I noticed a huge difference with him right away. No longer was he hanging his head low or avoiding eye contact. The stress that had been haunting him had disappeared from his face. I knew from his demeanor he had told Jill.

I swung the door open and ushered him in. "Hey man, good to see you. Come on in, I'm watching the game. Do you want a beer?"

Travis headed toward the couch. "A beer sounds good," he said, taking a seat. "Who's winning?"

"The Jets." I popped open a couple of beers and joined Travis in front of the screen. "I think they'll win this one."

Travis took one of the bottles from my hand and took a big swig. He smacked his lips. "Damn, thanks man. I needed that."

"So, how did it go last night?" I asked, after taking a generous gulp of my beer.

Travis leaned back into the couch, his knees apart, and took another swig. "Well, I told Jill, and she now hates me."

"Did you tell her everything, or just that you wanted to break up?"

"Oh, I told her everything and I fucked up, man." He took another long gulp and savored the taste. "I should never have cheated on her. Jill didn't deserve that. For a few years, we were good, and I should have respected her and broke up with her first, before doing the shit I did."

I never supported Travis when he told me he was seeing someone else, and now it seemed he was regretting it too. I could tell he needed to talk and get everything out in the open, so I let him.

"So, why did you?" I asked.

He tossed his head back against the cushion. "I don't know. It just sorta happened. I didn't plan on it. I knew Jill and I weren't going to last much longer and to be honest, I was fucking horny." Travis chugged on his beer. "Fuck! I told you, Jill and I hadn't had sex in over six months."

"Yeah, you did. But shit, dude, it didn't give you the green light to go fuck someone else." I glanced at the TV; another touchdown had been made by the Jets. "And I agree with you—you should have broken up with Jill first. But it's too late now. How did she take it?"

"Everything was cool, up until I told her about my new girl-friend. We probably would have left on good terms. She told me that she knew it was over for us, and was afraid to tell me because she wasn't sure if I felt the same way. But as soon as I mentioned I was seeing someone else, the shit hit the fan."

"Well, do you blame her?"

"No, I don't blame her. That's where I fucked up. She had a few choice words for me and told me to get out, and then she stormed upstairs."

"Yep, she went and met Sabela for lunch today."

Travis's jaw dropped and his head fell back against the cushions again. "Well, shit, that should be an interesting lunch. Now your girlfriend is going to hate me too."

"I'll be right back," I said, then left the room to grab two more beers. I returned a few minutes later, placing one in front of Travis on the coffee table.

"The Jets just scored another touchdown." Travis said, picking up the beer I just set down. "I think you're right about this game."

I ignored his comment about the game. "Listen, man. Sabela and I are caught up in the middle of this breakup of yours. Sabela has been friends with both of you since before I met her, and she went to dentist school with Jill before you started dating her. I don't know how all of this is going to pan out, but I'm sure we can all remain friends somehow."

Travis laughed.

"What's funny?" I asked.

He took another swig of his beer. "Well, you know how women can be when they get together. Sabela may ban me from coming here. After all, I did cheat on her girlfriend."

I shook my head. "Nah. Sabela is not the kind of woman to take sides." I was cut off by the front door opening. "Well, we're about to find out. She just got home," I said, using a quieter voice so I wouldn't be heard by Sabela.

Travis sunk lower into the couch and remained quiet.

After closing the door, she saw me sitting on the recliner, which was in view of the door, but didn't see Travis around the corner of the room. "Hey, babe. How was lunch?"

"Depressing," she said, kicking off her shoes. "Any more beers in the fridge?"

"Yeah. I just bought a twelve pack." I glanced over at Travis, who hadn't said a word.

From the living room, I heard the door of the fridge open and the sound of a beer being popped open.

"Fucking Travis. Why did he have to cheat on Jill?" she continued to talk while making her way to the living room. "I mean, what an asshole! I liked those guys as a couple. I liked hanging out with them. Now, because of stupid Travis, we can't do that anymore."

I found myself defending Travis. "I think their relationship was already over, babe. Even before he started seeing someone else."

Holding her beer in her hand, Sabela entered the living room and saw Travis sitting on the couch. "Travis! I didn't know you were here. That's okay, I'd still call you an asshole to your face," she said, before taking another sip of beer.

Travis raised his bottle. "That's okay, I deserve it. So, how's Jill holding up?"

Sabela sat at the other end of the couch. "That's a stupid question. How do you think she's holding up?" she asked, putting her feet up on the coffee table and sinking her body into the couch cushions. "She's okay with the breakup, Travis. It's the other woman she's upset about. God, what were you thinking?"

Travis spoke with a sharper tone. "Yeah, yeah, I fucked up. I was just telling Slater the same thing before you came home. But there's nothing I can do about it now but move on." He chugged his beer. "The damage is done. Jill will move on, and I'm sure she will find someone else real soon."

"Jill and I talked about our wedding. Slater and I want both of you there." Her eyes narrowed. "How's that going to be?"

Sabela had a good point. I hadn't thought about that, and I could tell from the disappointed look on Travis's face he hadn't either. It was funny how women thought about stuff that didn't even occur to us men.

"Shit, that might be a little awkward," I said, glancing over at Travis.

He stirred in his seat. There was no doubt the question made him uneasy. "Fuck, I don't know, Sabela. The wedding isn't here yet. Things should have calmed down by then. Geez, we just broke up last night."

"Well, I just hope you guys can be civil at our wedding. That's all I ask," Sabela said, using a firm voice.

Travis nodded. "Don't worry. Everything will be fine."

"So, where are you living now?" Sabela changed the subject and spoke in a softer tone.

Travis paused with the rim of his bottle almost touching his slightly parted lips. He took a swig, placed the bottle between his legs, and circled the rim with his finger. "I stayed at a hotel last night, but I hope to be moving in with my girlfriend," he said, looking down at his beer.

Sabela glanced my way, her eyes widening, before drilling Travis some more. "So, are you ever going to tell us who she is? Why are you keeping her secret?" Sabela looked my way again. "Right, Slater?"

"Yeah really, Travis. Why are you keeping us in the dark…do we know her?" I asked.

Unless my eyes were playing tricks on me, I could swear Travis was sinking lower into the couch and purposely avoiding eye contact with either one of us. "Travis?" I asked again.

Travis scrunched his eyes closed and twisted his face. "Fuck, man. Do we have to get into this right now?"

Sabela pulled her feet off the coffee table and sat up straight. "Why don't you want to tell us?"

Travis didn't answer.

"Travis? What's going on?" Sabela crossed her legs. "Are you going to keep us guessing? It's obvious to me that we must know her, from the way you're acting. I don't get it. Surely, she's not that bad," Sabela said with a crooked smile.

Travis jerked his head back and pulled at his hair by the handfuls. "Damn it, guys. I know you're gonna find out sooner or later, but I was hoping it was gonna be later." He pulled himself to an upright position, grabbed his beer, and took a deep swig. Sabela and I waited patiently for what he was about to tell us, glancing at each with puzzled looks, having no clue who the mystery woman might be.

Travis finished off his beer and looked my way. "Can I have another one?" he asked, setting down the empty bottle.

"Sure, man." I left the recliner to fetch him another drink and caught Sabela rolling her eyes.

Once back in my seat, and another opened beer in Travis's hand, Sabela wasted no time getting back to where we left off.

"Well, Travis. We're waiting," she said, folding her arms and crossing her legs. Her tone was sharp and forceful.

Travis glanced my way, then over at Sabela. There was an uncomfortable silence in the room and then he looked down. "It's Claire."

CHAPTER 18

SABELA

When Travis said his new girlfriend was Claire, I was not only shocked but horrified. I had to verify it was the Claire I knew. "Claire!" I screamed. "As in, Davin's sister?"

Travis avoided eye contact and instead looked down at his beer. "Yes."

"Oh fuck," was all Slater could manage to say, who was sitting quietly across from me.

As for me, I was seeing red and couldn't control my rage. The last time I felt this level of anger was when Davin had me arrested for stealing his car, which I never did.

I uncrossed my legs and glared at Travis. "Are you out of your fucking mind?" I hollered, feeling the muscles in my neck tighten. My eyes narrowed as I continued to stare him down but he wouldn't look at me. "Have you forgotten that Davin, her *brother*, tried to rape me?" I shook my head in disgust and scoffed. "What is fucking wrong with you, Travis? No wonder you didn't want to tell us." I looked over at Slater, who was speechless. "Can you fucking believe this?"

Slater shook his head. "I honestly don't know what to say. Why

Claire? You know what her brother did to Sabela." He shook his head again. "Fuck, Travis. I don't know if we can handle this one. I thought the way you broke up with Jill was bad enough. But this. Damn!"

As hard as I tried to fight them back, I couldn't stop the tears wallowing up in my eyes. I hadn't said Davin's name since I walked out of that courtroom. "How could you do this, Travis?" I said, tears now gushing down my cheeks. "I can't be friends with you while you're dating her. I'm sorry. I just can't do it."

Slater raised his hands, palms up. "Sorry, Travis, I have to agree with Sabela. I don't see how we can remain friends if you're dating the sister of Sabela's rapist."

Travis looked stunned. "Now, hold on a second, guys." He set down his beer. "Listen to yourselves. Claire is the sister. She didn't do anything wrong, except be the sister of a horrible man. Something she had no control over." Travis glanced my way with pity in his eyes. He spoke in a gentle tone, not taking his eyes off me. "Sabela, I'm sorry for what happened to you. It was an unforgivable act by a monster of man, but Claire did not do those things to you, and she shouldn't be treated like she did."

I wanted to listen to what he had to say and simply nodded while wiping away the last of my tears. I pulled myself together to ask him one question. "Does she talk or visit Davin? Because if so, that's another reason I can't be friends with you."

"As a matter of fact, no, she doesn't." He took a deep breath. "You probably don't know this, but she hasn't spoken to him since he was carted off to jail." He cracked a little smile. "She's disowned him, Sabela."

The news surprised me. "What about their parents?"

"Nope, she doesn't see them either, because they continue to defend him and make excuses for him. Claire has broken all ties with her family because of what he did to you."

I looked over at Slater, who sat with a blank face just like mine. Neither one of us knew what to say. I was numb and I could tell

Slater was too. "But she never liked me, Travis. When I worked with her, I always got the impression she hated me for dating Davin. So why would she care what Davin did to me. I honestly thought she'd get a kick out of it."

Travis gave me a warm smile, curling his lip just a tad in the process. "She never hated you, Sabela. If anything, she was jealous of you."

I creased my brow. "Jealous? Why?"

"For a number of reasons."

"Such as?" I asked.

"Well, look at you, you're gorgeous. Claire always use to compare herself to you and always felt like the plain Jane at the office. You're perfect in every way. Jill loves her bling and pinks, and has the bubbly personality to go with it. Do you remember how Claire dresses? She's self-conscious of her glasses." He glanced at both of us simultaneously. "Which I adore, by the way. She doesn't wear much makeup and her hair is short because she has no idea how to style it."

I was finding all this hard to believe. "She's told you all this?"

"Yes, she told me. Once you get to know her, Claire is the easiest person to talk to, and she's so real."

"Well, she never talked to me."

Travis cracked a little laugh. "That's because she was intimidated by you. She was by all of you. She didn't know how to strike up a conversation with any of you and so, kept to herself and did her work, taking x-rays all day. Her silence towards you had nothing to do with you dating Davin—she just didn't know how to be your friend."

While I listened to Travis, I could feel my anger slowly begin to subside and what was replacing it was pity. "Travis, I don't know what to say. I honestly thought she hated me."

Travis shook his head and took another swig of his beer.

"If Claire is so shy and quiet, how did you guys end up together?" I asked.

"It was at the dentist office. Jill wasn't answering her phone, and I had left my house keys at home and went by there to get hers, because she wasn't getting off for a few more hours." Travis laughed sarcastically. "Come to think of it, she hardly ever answered my calls. We hadn't been getting along for months before this happened. Anyway, when I parked my truck, I saw Claire crying in the car parked next to me. She turned the other way when I saw her."

"Then what happened?" I asked.

"Well, I'm not the kind of guy that ignores a girl who is alone and crying, so after getting out of my truck, I tapped on her window. I could tell she didn't want to, but she rolled down her window and I asked her if she was okay."

"What was wrong with her?' I asked, intrigued by his story.

Travis picked up his beer, took a long gulp, and leaned back against the cushions, keeping the beer in his hands. "Her car wouldn't start and after calling Triple A, they had told her she had used all her quoted tows for the year." He smirked. "I can see why. Her car has two-hundred-forty- thousand miles on it, and it kept breaking down."

I could see where his story was going. "So, you gave her a ride? Right?"

Travis nodded. "I figured out it was her starter and called a friend of mine who's a mechanic. His name is Brian. Do you know him?" he asked Slater.

Slater shook his head.

"Anyway, I knew Claire didn't have the money to fix it, so I paid Brian to come and fix it in the parking lot. He said it would take a couple of hours, so instead of getting keys from Jill, I invited Claire to lunch while we waited for her car."

"And what? You ended up in bed with her?" I asked with raised eyebrows.

Travis laughed. "No. We just started talking and poured our hearts out to each other." He gave me a serious stare." Sabela, I've never talked to anyone like that before. We just connected. We were both so honest with each other, and I can't explain it, but it felt right."

I was no longer feeling angry. I just wanted to know more about this unexpected relationship. "What did you guys talk about?"

"Oh god, everything. The first thing she said to me was, how could I talk to the sister of a rapist?"

"No!" I gasped.

"I'm not kidding, and from there, she just opened up about how she hates Davin for what he did, and it's because of him that she has no friends."

Listening to Travis was giving me goose bumps. While he was telling us the story, I'd glance over periodically at Slater, who was listening just as intently as me.

"The conversation led to me telling her about Jill and me. I told her everything and she even thanked me for my honesty," Travis said.

"What did you tell her?" I asked, letting curiosity get the better of me.

"I told her how we were so different, and that my attraction to Jill was purely physical. Claire understood when I explained to her that, during the whole time I was with Jill, I never really got to know her."

My brow creased again. "You didn't?"

Amused by my puzzled look, Travis grinned my way. "No, I never did because we never talked to each other. She's a self-absorbed person. If we did talk, it was always about her—what she wanted, what she didn't like, what I was doing wrong, or what she wanted me to buy her."

I must admit it stung a little when Travis talked about Jill that way, but I'd known Jill for a long time and he was right. Jill always had to be the center of attention. It was part of her personality and there was a guy out there somewhere that would cater to her every need and treat her like a queen, but Travis wasn't that guy. I nodded and let Travis continue.

"In the past month, I learned more about Claire than all the time I was with Jill, and do you know something?" He stared at Slater and me.

"No, what?" I asked.

"I knew at that very moment that it was over for Jill and I. Claire and I did nothing but talk for two hours and when I took her back to her car, I was sorry to see her go. I could have talked to her all night."

"So, when did you guys start seeing each other?"

Travis finished off his beer before telling us the rest of his story. "Well, after that, I couldn't stop thinking about her. She was like a breath of fresh air. A woman I could finally talk to about anything and she'd listen. After fixing her car, we exchanged phone numbers. I told her if she needed someone to talk to, to give me a call."

"And she did?" I asked.

"No. I knew Claire would never call me. She's too shy and has no confidence in herself. After two weeks went by, I called her and asked her how she was doing. I was sitting in my truck after work when I called, and we talked for an hour. I asked if she wanted to meet for a beer and she surprisingly said yes." A genuine relaxed smile appeared on Travis's face. "I was stoked, and called Jill right away to tell her I was working late and going out for beers with the guys."

"And that was it, eh?" I asked, before taking the last sip of beer from my bottle.

Travis nodded. "Yep. I went back to her place. After we had made love, she cried in my arms, worried about Jill and what she would do if she found out. Since then, I've told her I was going to end it with Jill. But as you know, it took a while."

I shook my head in disbelief. "How the hell did Claire manage to go to work while having an affair with you and being around Jill every day?"

"It was difficult for her, but then again, she's pretty good at keeping things to herself, as you now know. But after a month had gone by and I was still with Jill, Claire told me she couldn't do it anymore and I had to make a decision on what I was going to do." Travis sat up straight and placed his hands on his knees, his legs crossed at the ankles. "Well, that was it. I knew I had to end it with Jill, and I did last night."

Both Slater and I needed some time for Travis's story to sink in and had no words for a few seconds. Twenty minutes ago, I had felt nothing but rage toward Travis, but now I understood why their relationship had evolved. They were both seeking comfort and surprisingly, I thought it was sweet they had found each other, and I found myself no longer angered by the mention of Claire's name. I honestly believed I could be friends with her as soon as the dust has settled. My thoughts turned to Jill. "Do you plan on telling Jill?"

Travis shrugged his shoulders. "I know I should, but Claire is afraid of how she will act at work."

I understood and nodded. "I'd just get it over with. She has a right to know. Jill will be pissed I'm sure but, in all honesty, I think she'll get over it pretty quickly." I laughed. "She already asked me over lunch if I knew of any single guys."

"Really?" Travis asked with raised eyebrows. "Well, eventually, she will find out. I'm not obligated to give her reports on my future dating life."

I couldn't disagree with that. Travis had moved on, and I could tell he was relieved to tell us about Claire. I'm sure he was ready to explode, having to keep it to himself for a while. The stress lines were no longer visible around his eyes. In fact, they were the brightest they had been in a long time. It would take me some time to get use to the idea of Travis and Claire being a couple, but I sensed Travis's genuine happiness when he told us about her.

In time, Slater and I will have them over for dinner—but not yet. I wanted to get Eve's project behind us first. As for Jill, she was and always would be a close friend and I'd help her any way I could to get through this, but after lunch today, I could tell she was already beginning to move on.

I glanced at my watch and saw it was already after eight. "Well, guys, I'm beginning to feel the effects of the many beers I've had today, first with Jill and now you two." I rose to my feet. "I'm going to call it a day and enjoy a soak in the bath." I looked over at Travis, who was still sitting on the couch, and opened my arms. "Come give me a hug," I said with a warm smile.

Travis returned the smile and lifted himself off the couch to meet me in a hug.

"No hard feelings?" I asked.

Travis shook his head and smiled. "None."

"I'm happy for you guys," I told him while giving him a pat on the shoulder.

"Me too," Slater said, then looked in my direction. "I'll be up in a bit. I'm going to give Travis his check and fill him in on the Eve project."

I walked over to Slater, leaned over, and gave him a peck on the cheek. "Okay, sounds good." I paused and gave him a loving smile. "I'll see you soon."

CHAPTER 19

SLATER

It was a shock to hear about Travis and Claire, and I was quiet while he explained his attraction to her. It all made sense and I could see his eyes brighten whenever he mentioned her name. I knew his feelings were genuine and by the end of his visit, I too was happy for him.

How this would all pan out at our wedding though, I had no idea. I knew Sabela wanted Jill at the wedding, so I hoped everyone would just get along—at least on that day. But right now, I couldn't worry about it. It was Monday morning and Sabela and I were about to head over to Eve's place. I was expecting Travis to be there too, around nine. I'd hired him for the entire duration of the job and thanks to Eve, he would be paid well. I also talked to Drew and when we get to the drywall and painting stages, I was going to have Enrique and a couple of his guys come over and give us a hand.

Sabela wanted to handle the boy's bedroom and bathroom on her own, which was mainly cosmetic. Over the weekend, we picked out all the colors and spent a bunch of Eve's money online and in stores to complete the task. Sabela was eager to get started, and already had everything loaded in the truck we'd be driving over there by the time I had gotten dressed.

"Oh good, her car's not here," Sabela said as we pulled up to Eve's driveway. "Must mean she's out."

"Unless it's in the garage." I snickered.

Sabela nudged my elbow. "Oh hush. I've never seen her park in the garage."

"Do you have the keys?" I asked, after putting the truck in park.

She pulled them out of her jacket pocket and then picked up her phone. "Yeah, here you go. She also texted me instructions for the alarm," she said, searching on her phone. "Here it is. The code for the alarm is one-two-six-seven, and the keypad is by the front door."

"Okay. Got it," I said. "Let's go in and take a look around. Travis should be here soon."

We were greeted by the loud pitching sound of the alarm, and I immediately rushed over and punched in the code on the keypad to shut it off.

"Eve?" I called out, to make sure she wasn't here. She was not.

For a minute, Sabela and I stood in the entranceway and glanced around the fancy mansion.

"How much do you think this place is worth?" Sabela asked.

"Millions," I said.

She turned to face me. "Does it bother you that she has all this?"

I scanned the area where we stood and replied honestly. "No, it doesn't one bit. She may have all of this, but she has no one to share it with. That's really sad. Don't you think?"

"Yeah, I guess so. But fuck. Can you imagine living in a place like this? I'd get lost."

I laughed at her remark. "It would take some getting used to, but I'd much rather be poor and have the life I have with you over living here alone any day."

Sabela smiled and gave me a peck on the lips. "Aww, you say the sweetest things. I'm going to go check upstairs and see where I want to begin. Maybe when Travis gets here, you guys can help me unload the truck and take the stuff upstairs."

"Sure, not a problem. I'll be outside if you need me, or call me on my phone."

Twenty minutes later, I was standing in the yard with Travis, taking measurements, and jumped when I felt a tap on my back. "Shit, Sabela, you startled me."

She giggled at my fear. "Sorry," she said, followed by another snarky laugh.

"What's up?" I asked, while passing the tape measure to Travis.

Her tone softened. "Have you got a minute?" she asked with a concerned look.

"Yeah, of course." I turned to Travis. "I'll be right back."

He nodded. "Not a problem. I can get most of this on my own."

I followed Sabela into the house through the lower French doors, which led us into the unfinished basement. She handed me a piece of paper. "I found this on the kitchen bar."

I unfolded the note and read it out loud.

Dear Slater & Sabela,

I won't be home for the next four weeks or maybe longer. My sister has unexpectedly taken a turn for the worst. It doesn't look good. I will be staying with my mother and Scottie. So, you won't have to worry about me being here while you work. I did not have a chance to get you a credit card, so I am leaving you a book of signed checks. Use them for whatever you need. If you have any questions, you can text me.

Thank you,

Eve

After reading the note, an essence of sadness lingered over me. I had known her sister Loraine when I was dating Eve. I saw her at holiday gatherings, and there were a few times we had gone out for dinner with her and her new boyfriend at the time. I remembered her being much quieter than Eve. I suspected she was more like her late father who, I was told, was also reserved.

Eve was very much like her mother, who was a shallow person, hard to get to know, and her reputation was always a priority. She had to have the best of everything. Material items were what mattered to her—without them, she didn't feel adequate. I glanced around the mansion we were standing in. Yep, that was Eve.

I held the note loosely between my fingers and looked over at Sabela, whose expression was blank. "Wow. She's losing her sister."

"Yeah, I know." Sabela took the note and read it again. "It's kinda of hard to stay mad at her when she's going through this."

I was numb, unsure how to react. "Yeah, I know what you mean."

She took my hand. "Come on up to the kitchen. I want to show you the checks."

Just like the note said, the checkbook was on the counter. I flipped through the book. "Yep, she's signed every one of them," I said, after reaching the end of the checkbook.

Sabela folded her arms and leaned her lower back against the counter. "You know what I find weird?"

"No, what?" I asked, returning the checks to the counter.

"Well, I find it odd that she trusts us with a book of blank checks, but she locked the door to the master bedroom."

I raised my eyebrows. "She did?"

"Yeah. I'm sorry, but while I was upstairs, I did some snooping."

I looked at her with wide eyes. "Sabela!"

She shrugged her shoulders, giving herself a pass. "What? I'm only human. You'd do the same, I bet."

I was about to deny it, but she was right, I would have, and nodded instead. "Yeah, you got me. Well, did you find anything unusual?"

Sabela shook ahead. "No, but she must be hiding something. Why else would she lock her bedroom door?"

"Maybe she doesn't want us in her personal space." I tried to give her the easy solution, but she wasn't buying it. Before I finished, she was shaking her head.

"Nah. That's not it. This whole house is her personal space. I'm telling you, she's hiding something from us."

I didn't want to keep speculating with Sabela. My mind was clouded with the fact that Eve was losing her sister. No matter what she had done to me in the past, I was feeling compassion for her during what must be a difficult time right now. I wanted to end this conversation, and spoke with a sharp tone.

"Sabela, can we not talk about this right now? Even if she is hiding something, who cares? It's her life." I took her hand. "What bothers me is that it sounds like Lorraine is dying. She's only a few years older than Eve. Would it bother you if I texted Eve and told her how sorry I am?"

Sabela's face became flushed, and she squeezed my hand. "No, of course I don't mind." She ran her fingers through her hair, pulling it back, away from her face. "I don't know why I'm so wrapped up in Eve's business. Tell her I'm sorry too."

"I will, and if she replies, I'll let you know what she says." I could see the uneasiness in Sabela's face when I mentioned texting Eve. I squeezed her hand again and pulled her in. "I have nothing to hide when it comes to Eve. I want you to know that."

Sabela nodded.

I kissed her softly on the lips. "This doesn't change the way I feel about her. I still don't trust her, and I never will. I just think this is the right thing to do."

Sabela kissed me back. "You don't have to explain. I agree with you." She patted me on my shoulders with both hands. "Now, I'm going to go back upstairs and continue on with my project. I'm starting in the bedroom first." She gave a satisfactory smile. "It's going to look so cute when it's done."

She paused for a moment and stepped away, then looked at me with distinct sadness in her eyes. "It just dawned on me that Scottie is about to lose his mother. Oh, that poor little boy." She held her hand up to her lips and sniffed back a tear. "How could I be so selfish? I wonder if he will be living here permanently with Eve?"

The thought had never occurred to me. I was so wrapped up trying to comprehend her sister was dying, I hadn't even thought about her nephew. "Oh damn. I forgot about her son." My heart felt heavy, knowing he would soon be without a mother. I was lost for words. "Maybe," was all I could manage to say.

Sabela folded her arms. "Do you think Eve knew her sister was dying?" She didn't wait for my answer. "I think she did." Sabela paced around the kitchen in small circles, her brow creased. "I believe she'll be bringing Scottie back here to live with her. That's why she wants us to finish the job as quickly as we can, because she knows her sister doesn't have much time."

I rubbed my brow deep. "I don't know what to think." I glanced at my watch. "Let's get back to work. I'll text Eve later." I gave Sabela a peck on the cheek. "I love you."

"I love you too," she said with a soft smile before leaving the kitchen.

I didn't mention any of the disturbing news about Eve and her sister to Travis—only because I didn't know how. I was still trying to understand all of this myself. The news was so sudden, and was Sabela right. *Did Eve know last week that her sister was dying?"* If all of Sabela's predictions were correct, I now understood Eve's urgency to finish this job in the shortest amount of time possible. The question was, could we cut it even shorter?

CHAPTER 20

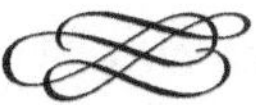

SABELA

Over the next few weeks, everyone worked hard on Eve's project, to finish the job sooner than the anticipated deadline of three months. We were hoping to shave off a month, and hired extra help though Drew. Instead of hiring three extra guys, we hired six. One of those was Ricky, who Slater and I shamelessly embarrassed by making out in one of the condos we were all working on—knowing he was watching.

After that devious stunt we pulled, poor Ricky couldn't look me in the eye for the remaining time we worked together. But now, over a year later, he didn't have a problem.

On his first day, he arrived at Eve's with his head held high and a noticeable confidence in his stride. The transformation was uncanny. He had grown his hair, which now rested on his shoulders, parted in the middle, and swept away from his face. And I wanted to say he had blond highlights done, but I didn't want to ask.

When he shook my hand, his grip was strong and forceful. For a moment, I was speechless. Was this the same Ricky? He wore a white t-shirt and I couldn't help noticing his muscular, tanned arms. When I last saw him, he was a skinny, pale kid. Now, he was a cute—no, a sexy young man.

"Wow! Look at you, Ricky," I had said to him during our unexpected handshake. He had smiled, and I was taken back by how gorgeous his grin was and how white his teeth were.

When he spoke, he looked directly into my eyes, never once shying away like he used to.

"Hello, Sabela. It's good to see you." His voice was calm, his words defined.

I was stunned for a few seconds, holding his hand a little longer than I should have.

"Ricky, you look great," was all I could think to say.

He had given himself the once-over and smiled. *"Thanks. I owe it all to you and Slater."*

I creased my brow. *"You do? What do you mean?"*

I remembered his explanation clearly, and it made me realize how lucky I was. *"When I saw you and Slater making out that day, it made me take a good look at myself. I wanted what you two had. What I saw was real. Two people in love, who weren't afraid to express it."* I remembered his slight chuckle at that point. *"And share with others, I might add."*

I had blushed at his remark.

"At first, I was so embarrassed that I had watched you but when I got home, I took a good look at myself in the mirror and didn't like what I saw." He had laughed again. *"No wonder I'd not had a girlfriend in over two years. I was a skinny dork. From that day on, I've never looked back and began doing things to improve myself, and I've never felt better."*

I had asked him if he had found a girlfriend.

"I've had a few but I'm still searching for the right one."

Right away, Jill came to mind. She'd already hinted she was ready to date again. Soon, I'd suggest a double date with Slater and I, but I needed to check with Jill first.

~

By the end of the fourth week, Scottie's bedroom and bathroom were complete and looked adorable. They turned out exactly how I had pictured, with the train theme, a railway track, and model train circling the entire room.

The outside play area was near completion and work had begun on the unfinished basement. Slater and I had been working weekends since we started the job, in the hopes of getting it done quicker, but this weekend, we decided to take it off and relax for a change, which was long overdue.

"So, what do you want to do this weekend?" Slater asked on Saturday morning. He was stretched out on the couch, drinking his first cup of coffee.

I stirred my freshly brewed cup and took a seat on the wide arm of the couch.

"Wanna go to the beach?" I asked. "It's supposed to be a hot one today. I could do with a swim in the ocean, and maybe you can finally give me some of those surfing lessons you've been promising me."

Slater sat up and made room for me next to him. I slid my body off the arm and onto the softer cushion.

"That's a great idea! Working over at Eve's has been kinda of depressing. I keep thinking about that poor kid."

"Yeah, me too," I replied, before taking my first sip of coffee.

"I think the beach will do wonders for us." His eyes lit up and a massive grin appeared on his face. "Better yet..."

"Better yet, what?" I asked.

He nudged my arm, the one holding my coffee, and I steadied my cup to prevent a spill. The large grin appeared again as he spoke. "We could go see if Susie and Vic are at the beach today. They said they are always there on Saturdays," he said with a smirk.

This time, I had a large devious grin. "Oh wow! Now, that

could be fun." I snickered as I nuzzled my head into the crook of his neck.

Slater curled his arm over my shoulder and pulled me in closer. He kissed the top of my head gently and whispered, "I think it will be a lot of fun."

I smiled. "Me too."

"As soon as we're done with our coffee, we'll get dressed and load up the car, okay?"

I turned to face him and met him in a soft, sensual kiss. "Sounds good." I licked my lips, savoring his taste, then whispered, "This may be a good weekend after all."

It turned out the nude beach was only forty minutes from our condo. Who knew! We parked our truck in the allocated parking lot—which, to my surprise, was almost full—and I looked around, then laughed. "Damn, I had no idea there were so many nudist in the San Diego area."

"If I read it correctly online, the south end of the beach is clothing optional only," Slater said before stepping out of the truck.

"Ahh, okay. That makes sense."

While Slater retrieved his surfboard from the bed of the truck, and the ice chest, which thankfully was on wheels, I grabbed our beach bag and towels from the back seat. The parking lot was a busy place. Surfers were returning to their vehicles, carrying their boards under their arms after an early morning surfing session. Others were taking advantage of the installed fresh water showers, and off to the left, I saw a trail busy with people.

"I guess that's the way to the beach," I said, pointing.

He looked in the direction I was staring. "Looks like it. Are you ready?" he asked as he flung his wetsuit over his board and wedged both under his arm.

"Yep." I grinned. "I've never been to a nude beach before. Have you?"

"Nope, this will be a first for me too." He chuckled. "Come on, let's go."

The trail was long and steep down to the beach. "I guess they want to keep the nudists hidden," I said, after a good five or ten-minute hike. Then, we finally saw the end of the trail in sight. "I'm not looking forward to the walk back to the car."

Slater, who was a few steps in front of me, turned his head slightly. "Oh, it will be good for you."

When we reached where the trail met the sand, a prominent sign was posted. It had an arrow pointing to the left, with the words: *Clothing Optional.*

"Guess we go that way," Slater said, adjusting his surfboard under his arm.

I glanced ahead and saw, not ten feet from where we were standing, a naked guy walking our way. I felt myself blush when my eyes instantly zoned in on his junk—thank god I was wearing my shades. As he passed by, I didn't know where to look and simply nodded. Slater did the same.

"Well, that was awkward," I said, standing close to Slater, unable to hold his hand because of the bags and towels I was carrying.

"Just a bit." Slater nodded.

As we made our way down the beach, we kept close to the edge by the rocks, where there were less crowds but still, we passed more naked people. Some were single guys. Others were couples holding hands as they strolled passed us. All comfortable with their bodies—whether they were too skinny, too fat, no boobs, or big boobs. No one was judging anyone. As we walked by, everyone nodded, some even said hi. It was odd that, even though I was dressed in my usual beach attire—cut-off shorts and white two-piece bathing suit—I felt overdressed. Funny, I was now anxious to take off my clothes and join these liberated people and experience it for myself.

"Keep an eye out for their umbrella. What was on it again?" Slater asked.

"A big blue one with yellow smileys," I told him. "They said we couldn't miss it." As soon as I said that, I spotted it, up by the rocks, away from the general population of the beach. I pointed with my finger. "There it is. They're here."

Slater followed my hand with his eyes and saw them. "Ahh, okay. Yep, definitely can't miss that umbrella." He laughed and scanned the area where we stood. "Okay, now we gotta find a spot...but I don't want it to be too obvious. I don't want them to know we're here."

"Me neither," I said.

Together, we glanced up and down the beach, still shocked by seeing everyone naked and doing what people normally do on the beach, except with no clothes on—sunbathe, volleyball, Frisbee, and swimming. After a few minutes, Slater found the perfect spot, about fifty feet away from Susie and Vic.

Hidden behind my shades, I glanced their way, but I couldn't see their faces. They were both lying down on their stomachs. One of his hands was resting on one of her butt cheeks. From what I could see, they both looked to be in excellent shape. Both were tanned. Susie had long, auburn hair tied into a ponytail while his was short and black.

"Do you see them?" I asked Slater.

"Yeah, we got a good view from here."

In front of us, about seventy feet away, was another couple. The woman was wearing a big floppy sunhat and the guy was lying face down next to her, so I couldn't see either of their faces. I wondered if they were here to watch them too.

"You know what I want to do?" I giggled.

"What?" Slater asked.

"Swim in the ocean naked with you. I've never done it and I think it would be such a rush."

"I'll race you," Slater yelled, stripping down.

"You're on!" And with no second thoughts or hesitations, I striped down to nothing and began running toward the water. I couldn't believe I was running on a public beach naked—it felt fucking awesome. Feeling the breeze in places I hadn't before tickled my nerves. I glanced over my shoulder, where Slater was right behind me, and his large grin told me he was feeling the same way. We ran into the water together, falling into the crashing waves with a powerful feeling of freedom that was new and exhilarating.

"This is fucking amazing!" I screamed, tossing my hair back and wiping the salt water out of my eyes. I looked over at Slater, who was standing in the surf, laughing. "Hey, are you going to surf naked?"

Slater glanced out to the horizon. "I don't think there's any surfing here, only on the other side," he called back.

"Well, that sucks. I would love to have watched you," I said, right before another wave crashed over my head.

Slater came to my rescue and pulled me to my feet. I laughed as I cleaned the salt water off my face and stood for a moment, watching all the naked people around me. I was fascinated at how everyone was at ease, smiling and laughing.

Slater approached me and pressed his muscular, drenched body against mine. "How are you doing?" he asked, his arms circling my waist.

"I've never felt better. I never knew nudism could be so much fucking fun. Look at these people," I said, gesturing around us.

Slater threw back his head and laughed before pulling me in for a wet, salty kiss. He kissed me hard, forcing his tongue between my lips. I didn't resist and welcomed the taste into my mouth. While kissing me, he slid a hand beneath the water and up between my legs. I gasped from his touch and gasped again when two of his fingers entered me. "Oh fuck, Slater!" I said, between breaths of air, my words muffled.

He broke away from our kiss and pushed his fingers deeper into me. I struggled to contain myself and my sounds of pleasure while trying to grasp what I was doing. *Here I am, naked in the ocean, being finger fucked beneath the surface while surrounded by dozens of naked people, who have no idea what Slater is doing to me.* What a friggin' turn on this was.

He kissed me again, but even harder, then quickly pulled back, leaving me breathless and wanting more.

"I so want to do you right now," he whispered in my ear." Let's go over to our towels and see what happens. Maybe we can get Susie and Vic to watch us."

After Slater had freed his fingers, he grabbed my hand and led me to shore. His strides were long and quick, and I trotted to keep up with him. Once we reached our spot, he turned to me and smiled. "God, you look awesome naked on the beach."

I gave him the onceover and chuckled. "You're not so bad yourself," I said, moving in closer and pressing my body against his. My left hand was between us, hidden, and discreetly, I squeezed his manhood. "I love seeing your cock dangling free." I laughed.

He gave his hips a quick thrust before giving me a playful bite on the neck, causing me to twist my body and squeal.

"Come on, let's lay down. I want to put some oil on you," he said, followed by that gorgeous smile that always melted my heart.

I glanced around our surroundings. The other couples had left, but Susie and Vic were still there. This time, they had rolled over on their backs. Susie was sitting up and she giggled while letting her hair down. She shook her head vigorously and then leaned down to kiss Vic. I felt a spark as I watched her and found myself wanting her to do more—maybe reach down between his legs. I was definitely turned on by what I was seeing, and hoped they'd watch us.

I lay face down on the towel, looking in their direction. My legs were slightly apart, my arms bent at the elbow, serving as a head-rest. I released a subtle moan as I felt the warmth of the sun soothe my bare ass and the slight breeze travel up between my legs.

"Man, this feels good," I said, my eyes closed.

Slater took a moment to brush the sand off my skin, using light feathery strokes. "Your body is so perfect. I could look at it all day," he murmured, brushing off the last of the sand before reaching for the bottle of oil.

I giggled. "It's yours to look at whenever you want."

A few seconds later, I felt a pool of warm oil in the center of my back and then streaks of it run down my legs. I moaned as it trickled down the surface of my skin.

"Ahh yes," I whispered, anticipating Slater's touch.

Working on my back first, he kneaded the oil into my skin with deep, massaging strokes. I felt myself sinking from his touch. I subtly looked over at Susie and Vic, and saw Susie was watching us while nudging Vic. I held my breath, anticipating his reaction, and then released a satisfactory smile when he rolled over to take a look.

"They're looking this way," I whispered, as Slater moved his hands down to my thighs.

"They sure are," Slater murmured. "Turn over. I want them to watch me rub oil over your immaculate breasts."

I didn't need to be told twice and was on my back in a matter of seconds. I propped myself up on my elbows and scanned the beach to make sure we weren't drawing any negative attention. We were not. No one seemed to notice but Susie and Vic.

Slater turned his head away and stared at them. "They're still watching us," he said before pressing his naked body against mine and kissing me passionately on the lips. I opened my mouth and searched for his tongue, kissing him hard and enjoying the taste of his breath. He kissed me harder, our lips locked tight. Not letting go, Slater straddled me, his legs bent at the knees. I caved beneath his weight, allowing my head to rest on the towel. Slater didn't stop; he kissed me with a greater force, pushing my head into the sand.

"Fuck! I'm so fucking turned on right now," he panted between breaths while reaching for the oil next to us.

Waiting for his next move, I reached up and spread my palms over his chest, enjoying the fine moist hairs tickling my skin.

"I want you," I moaned before looking over at our neighbors. "Look, he's putting oil on her breasts." I watched as she arched her back. "God, that is so fucking hot to see."

Slater poured a generous amount of oil over my breasts and now prominent nipples. I gasped at the sudden heated sensation and arched my back, just like I had seen Susie do.

Still straddling me, Slater worked the oil into my chest using deep circular motions, teasing my nipples with a delicate touch before pinching and squeezing them hard. With my eyes closed, I moaned repeatedly, absorbing his touch and yearning for him to be inside me.

Slater continued to rub my breasts while looking over at Susie and Vic. "He's now kissing her and she's spreading her legs," Slater whispered.

I strained my neck to see and was mesmerized by the view. They looked good together. They were in tune with each other's needs, like Slater and me. While watching them, I felt a tingling sensation between my legs. I was itching to be filled.

"Kiss my breasts," I whispered to Slater.

After a quick scan of the beach, he fulfilled my request and locked his mouth over my left nipple, burying his face into my flesh. I shrieked and pushed his head firmly onto my chest, holding it there with both palms as he continued to caress my boob with his mouth. I arched my back again, wanting him to take as much as he could into his mouth. I wriggled beneath him, and let go of his head so I could reach down and squeeze his muscular thighs that rested on either side of me.

Slater slid his head over to my other breast, his face disappearing into my rounded mound. I dug my nails into his thighs, causing him to wince. Images of the other couple entered my head, and I turned to take another look. He was kissing her stomach now and she was looking this way. Turned on that she was watching us, I pulled Slater's head up by his hair.

"Kiss me," I moaned.

He did as I asked and I pulled him in closer, locking strands of his hair between my fingers.

Slater sneaked a peak at the couple while kissing me, then hastily broke away, lifting himself off my body.

"Spread your legs," he said, panting.

I obeyed without any reservation and in an instant; Slater rolled his body back on top of mine. This time, his legs were straight, pressing in between my slightly parted ones. I embraced him with my arms, expecting him to kiss me, but he had other plans. In one swift movement, and with his chest heaving, he reached around with both hands and unhooked himself from my grasp, pinning my arms above my head. I smiled, liking the force he was using. He kissed me, pushing his tongue into my mouth. I kissed him back, exploring the roof of his mouth with mine.

"I'm going to make love to you right here," he whispered, his hot breath saturating my sinuses.

I nodded.

He lowered his head and sucked on my neck before gliding his tongue down between my breasts. Unable to move, my body became tense from his teasing touches. He paused and looked up. "But you have to contain yourself when you want to come." He gave my nipple a sensual stir with his tongue. "No one can know what I'm doing to you." He turned and looked at Susie and Vic. "Except them."

I nodded. I was aching for him to enter me. I tried to raise my hips but Slater's weight on top me wouldn't allow it. Still holding my hands above my head, Slater began to slowly gyrate his hips across my hips. His throbbing erection brushed against my thighs, teasing me some more. He looked over at the couple. Vic was in the same position as himself, on top of Susie, kissing her. Slater knew Vic was entering her at that moment, by the way she opened her legs just a little more to welcome him.

"Guess what?" Slater moaned.

I took a few deep breaths. "What?"

"He's fucking her right now."

My chest heaved and my heart raced. "Do it!" I said between breaths.

Slater was so hard, he didn't need to guide his cock in with his hand. With ease, I felt the tip slide between my legs. I adjusted myself and spread my legs a little further, and then he was in. I released a long, loud satisfactory moan as I felt myself melt beneath him.

Slater covered my mouth with his hand. "Shh. No sounds, remember."

"Then kiss me."

Slater released my hands, allowing me to lock them around his neck and pull his face to mine.

Slippery from the oil, our bodies glided together in a slow rhythmic movement. I moaned, feeling him use gentle subtle thrusts to reach deeper into my core. After each thrust, he squeezed my hips and rode my body with ease.

"God, you feel good." He moaned.

It was a gentle subtle lovemaking that curled my toes. I looked over at Susie and Vic and saw they were in the exact same position as us. Slowly, he rode his body over hers while looking our way. He knew we were watching—I could tell.

Slater took a nipple into his mouth and gently licked it in a circular motion. The sensation sent me over the edge. My body became tense and Slater knew I was about to climax.

"Come on, baby," he whispered before covering my mouth with his.

Pressing his hips firmly into mine, he pushed himself deeper and kept himself there as my body struggled to jolt from the electrifying orgasm I was having. With his mouth pressed firmly against mine, preventing any sounds to escape, I released what muffled screams I could into his mouth as he held my body still with his.

While my orgasm was still trying to find a way to escape, Slater's body stiffened and with one final gentle, discreet push, he emptied his juices into me, muffling his moan within our ongoing kiss. For some time, we allowed our bodies to relax from the magical sensations we had just experienced.

When we parted our lips, I lifted my head, slightly, and buried it into Slater's chest. I giggled. "Holy shit! What is wrong with us?"

Slater laughed while stroking my hair. "Nothing. We just know how to have a good time."

I turned my head and saw the couple was now lying side by side. "They must have come too." I snickered. "I would love to have seen that."

Slater pulled himself off me and rolled his body onto the empty space of the towel.

"Well, nothing says we can't come back," he said.

"True." I nodded.

I admired Slater as he stretched out his body and placed one arm under his head while stroking my thigh with the other. His body glistened from the oil.

"Damn, I could let you fuck me all day," I said with a devious smile.

"Careful what you wish for," he said with a smirk. "I just might."

I chuckled and rested my head on his chest. "Do you think we're weird?"

"What?" Slater spoke in a sharper tone. "Don't be silly. We just know how to have fun."

"That was pretty cool. As soon as I knew they were watching us, it was like a switch went on and I couldn't turn it off." I lifted my head to face him. "I get so turned on when I know someone is watching us. And then, just now, watching them was like the icing on the cake. I've never watched someone have sex before—it was beautiful. I now know what we give to others." I paused. "And do you know what I really like about it?"

Slater stroked my hair, pushing it back over my shoulder. "No, what?"

"I don't know why, but I have no desire to talk to or get to know that couple. Is that wrong of me?"

"Not at all. It makes perfect sense. I feel the same way. We both like the anonymity of the whole thing. I mean, can you imagine doing this sort of thing with say, Travis?"

I jumped up from his chest. "Eww. Hell, no!" I shrieked.

Slater laughed again. "See? Doesn't have the same effect, does it? That's why you don't want to know these people." He glanced over to the couple. "And see. Looks like they feel the same way. They're not coming over here, wanting to introduce themselves. They had their kicks and now they are simply lying in the sun next to each other." Slater jabbed my ribs with his index finger. "Don't overthink it. You're not weird. Just enjoy it."

"You're right," I said, tossing my hair back and giving him a loving smile. "Hey, wanna go for another swim?"

He smiled back. "You bet," he replied. "I love seeing you naked in the ocean."

CHAPTER 21

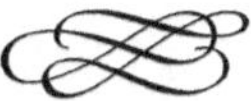

SLATER

e were now five weeks into the job and the entire time, Eve had only texted me once, and that was in the beginning, to let me know she may be gone for six weeks. I wasn't worried and I didn't want to bother her, especially knowing what she was going through with her sister. Her checks were clearing. Everyone was getting paid and supplies were being delivered on time. It was all falling into place and it looked like we would be able to wrap up the job in another three weeks, which would be a month ahead of schedule. Pleased with our progress, I sent a text to Eve with the good news.

Three days went by with no reply. "Do you think it's odd that Eve hasn't answered my text?" I asked Sabela while we were adding the finishing touches to the power wheels racetrack in the outside playing area.

Sabela hooked the last piece of black chain to the post. "Yeah, I do. But then again, everything she does is odd. She's not been here the whole time. That, to me, is strange." She stood back and admired our work. "Looks good," she said with a nod. "We also have no idea what she's going through," Sabela added, handing me a box of screws. "She may not want to deal with this right now."

"Yeah, I guess you're right," I replied with a nod.

Sabela knelt and picked up the rest of the unused chain with both hands. "Come on, let's go to lunch. I'm starving." She walked through the gate of the little white picket fence we had built around the play area. She stopped and turned to face me, holding out the chain. "Where shall I put this?"

I pointed to a spot to the left, close to the driveway. "Over there is fine."

She placed the chain in the designated spot and slid her hands into her back pockets. "Do you want to ask anyone else to join us for lunch?" she asked.

"Nah. It will take another half hour to round everyone up. I'm starving, and want to get back here and finish up this area by the end of the day."

~

We decided to go to Coco's. It was the closest, cheapest restaurant, but still a twenty-five-minute drive from Eve's upscale neighborhood. Even though we were making good money and had money in the bank after our bills had been paid, our spending habits hadn't changed. Paying over eighty dollars for a lunch for two people just seemed insane. We had checked out a place close to Eve's, and ate there only once. Not only was it over-priced and overrated, it took over thirty minutes for them to bring us our food, and the whole time, they were trying to sell us alcohol while we waited. The food wasn't that good and when we left, we were still hungry because the portions were so small, served on fancy white plates, with more garnish than the entree. Our wardrobe didn't help either. Dressed in our work clothes, many snubbed their noses at us, including the staff, I might add. We didn't leave a tip.

We were halfway through our burger and fries when my phone rang. I picked it up and saw it wasn't a number I recognized, but then, I've been getting a lot of calls from unknown numbers while doing Eve's job and decided to take the call, in case it was work-related.

"Slater here."

There were a few seconds of silence before I heard a female on the other end. "Hello, Ian. It's Patricia."

She called me Ian, so I knew right away, it was someone I hadn't spoken to in a long time. Ian was a name I no longer used unless it was official business.

"Ian? Are you there?"

It took me a minute to realize who the woman was. She was Eve's mother. "Patricia." My voice was flat—I sensed this was not going to be a pleasant call. Patricia tolerated me, but she never grew fond of me while I was with Eve. She once told me in confidence that Eve was being held back because of me and I would never be able to give her what she deserved in life. She even went on to tell me that I shouldn't be selfish, and let Eve go.

"Hello, Ian. It's important that I see you."

I became concerned. "Is everything okay, Patricia?"

"I don't want to talk over the phone." I heard her sniff back a tear. Her voice sounded broken. "Can we meet today?"

I glanced at my watch and then over at Sabela, who picked up on my concerned tone. I shrugged my shoulders at her. "Sure, Patricia. What time and where?"

"Can I come to your home? Where it is quiet, and not many people around us."

I looked over at Sabela again as I spoke. "Sure, you can come to our house."

Sabela gave me a puzzled look and whispered, "Who is it?"

I held up my hand to halt her questions for a moment. "Here's our address, Patricia." I listened while she read it back to me. "What time can we expect you?"

"Would five o'clock be okay? It's quite a drive from my house. And will your fiancée be there?"

"Yes, she will."

"Good. It's important that she is."

"Okay. Then we'll see you at five."

After thanking me, Patricia hung up and I looked at Sabela with a blank stare. "Well, that was weird."

"Who was that?" Sabela asked anxiously.

"It was Eve's mother." I shook my head. "I've not talked to her in years."

"What does she want?"

"I don't know. She wants to meet us at our house tonight at five."

Sabela leaned back in the booth, her brow creased. "You're right, that is weird. Do you think it has something to do with Eve?"

"Well, what else could it be?"

"Maybe her sister passed away," Sabela suggested, resting her elbows on the table.

"But why call me?" I was baffled. "And if that's the case, why didn't *Eve* call me?"

Sabela nodded. "True. Maybe she's too distraught."

"And her mother's not? I don't know, I guess we'll find out tonight. In the meantime, let's finish up and get back to work. I need to tell Travis we're leaving early and he's in charge."

Five o'clock sharp, our doorbell rang. Patricia had always been punctual, and I saw things hadn't changed. Always feeling belittled by her in the past, I made the effort when I got home to shower and change out of my work clothes, and put on a clean pair of jeans and a crisp white dress shirt. Sabela did the same and came down the stairs, wearing a cute flowery summer dress.

"You look great." I smiled before opening the door.

Sabela made her way to the kitchen where she had coffee brewing, and desserts. I opened the front door and found myself standing before a woman who hadn't changed in the last five years. I couldn't see her eyes, but I sensed she had been crying, explaining the sunglasses she was wearing. Her hair was how I remembered it, blonde, not her natural color because her black roots were showing. The style was the same, short and layered away from her face.

Hanging from her ears were her infamous bold earrings—these were black oval ones with gold edging. She was wearing more makeup than I recall, maybe because her skin was probably showing signs of weathering from age. She must be close to sixty by now. She had expensive taste and her wardrobe showed it. I knew everything she wore was a name brand, from her black pants and black sweater to her black pumps. She was wearing a diamond pendant and an expensive-looking oversized black purse hung from her shoulders.

"Patricia, it's been a long time." I motioned her in with my arms. "Come in. Sabela just made some coffee."

She removed her shades and walked in. Yes, she had been crying. "Hello, Ian," she said, tucking her sunglasses into her purse.

There was an uncomfortable silence while Patricia sized up our place. "You have a nice home."

"Thank you," I replied, leading her over to the dining room table. I pulled out a chair. Sabela stood in the kitchen and walked over to me. I wrapped an arm around her waist. "This is my fiancée, Sabela."

"Hi," Sabela said. "Would you like some coffee?"

"That would be great. Thank you," Patricia replied as she placed her purse on the table.

I took a seat across from her, placing my forearms on the table and locking my hands together in front of me. "So, what's this about?" I asked.

Before answering, she reached into her purse and pulled out a silk handkerchief, then gently dabbed her eyes. "Eve passed away three days ago."

Stunned, I shook my head in disbelief. "What?"

Sabela echoed my words. "What?" and dashed to the table with Patricia's coffee. After setting it in front of her, she took a seat next to me.

"What do you mean, she passed away? I thought Loraine was sick."

Patricia dabbed her eyes once more; the tears were becoming more frequent. "Is that what she told you?"

"Yes." I took Sabela's hand and held it tight. "Why would she lie to us?"

"There was a lot she didn't tell me, and I think before I say any more"—she reached into her purse and pulled out a white manila envelope—"you should read this."

I took the envelope from her hands. "What's this?"

"She left it for you, and one for me and one for Scottie, with strict instructions they not be opened until after she had passed. They remained on her dresser where she could see them."

Still numb from the news, I opened the envelope with care and glanced at the neatly typed letter that began with, *Dear Ian.* I turned and looked at Sabela. Her head rested on my shoulder, and our hands—now in my lap—were locked. I placed the letter in front of us on the table and together, we read the letter in silence.

Dear Ian,

You may hate me after reading this, but I've tried the best I could to clean up my messes before I leave this world—which shouldn't be long now. I'm doing what's best for Scottie. I'm going to start from the beginning and fill in all the blanks.

First of all, I'm sorry for hurting you. I was a fool for leaving you and thinking I could find something better. They always say you never know what you had until it's gone. It's true, believe me. You remember how it was—I was always complaining about what I didn't have.

I released a slight chuckle at her honesty and then continued reading.

Well, I met David online and he promised me the world. He was a real estate tycoon, and a wealthy one at that. He sent me pictures of one of his houses and his jet. He told me he would buy me whatever I wanted and I fell for it. I looked around our little house and told myself I wanted more, and that was it—I told him to buy me a ticket to New York, where he lived, and I left you. Again, I'm sorry.

In the beginning, he treated me like a queen. We lived in a huge mansion, I had servants and he bought me anything I wanted and took me to faraway exotic places. I'm not going to lie – I was happy for a while, and so was my mother. I thought I was living the fairytale.

I glanced over at Patricia, who remained silent and took a sip of her coffee. I said nothing and returned to reading the letter.

That was, until I discovered I was pregnant. I didn't tell David at first. He was off someplace around the world, and I went and saw the doctor on my own. My period had stopped three months prior but I kept putting off going to the doctors, hoping I'd get it. But I didn't. I had gained a little bit of weight but not much. But when my doctor told me I was six months pregnant, the math didn't add up. I'd only been with David for four months. I knew then I was already pregnant when I had left you. I just didn't know it at the time. Ian, you must believe me when I tell you—I would never have left you if I had known I was pregnant. Little Scottie is your son.

"What!" I had to read the words again out loud. "Little Scottie is your son, our son, not my nephew, like I led you to believe." I turned to Sabela. "Oh my god, why didn't she ever tell me?"

Sabela rubbed my arm, tears trickling down her cheeks. "I don't know. My god, Slater, you're his father."

I was too emotional to reply. My hands were trembling and my heart was racing. I kept repeating the words over in my head: Scottie was my son.

"Keep reading. She explains why she never told you," Patricia said between her tears. "I just found out myself in the letter she wrote to me. I had no idea he was your son either, Ian. But there's no denying it, he's the spitting image of you."

I wiped away a tear that had escaped my eye and read more of Eve's confession.

There was no way I could come crawling back to you after what I had done to you, so I told David that Scottie was his son. I knew at least he would be taken care of and would never go without anything. Yes, he did the right thing and married me. But only to protect his image, I'm sure of it.

Shortly after our well-publicized wedding, he became an arrogant, selfish asshole. He wasn't even there for the birth of Scottie. He was in Jamaica—probably with a girl on each arm. At the hospital, I had your name put on the birth certificate—David didn't deserve the title of father, and I knew he would never ask to see it.

I never saw him much after Scottie was born. I stayed behind with my son while he partied and carried on like a single man. His only advice when it came to Scottie was that he should be put in a boarding school when he turned three.

I was diagnosed with terminal brain cancer last year and was given about a year to live. I never told David and knew I couldn't leave Scottie with him, and demanded a divorce. We agreed on a settlement, which he couldn't have written up fast enough. He wanted nothing to do with Scottie and pretty much paid me off to just go away.

I left and came back to California to find you. I wanted to make sure Scottie would be with his father once I had passed. I bought my house with the intentions of leaving it to you and Scottie. When I met you, I saw the rage in your eyes and didn't know how to begin telling you about your son. I had already made up the story about my sister being his mother to Sabela, because I didn't want to tell her that you were his father without you being there. In the end, I chickened out completely, and am now leaving you this letter.

I'm happy you have found a good woman. I know you and Sabela will take care of Scottie, and I know Sabela will treat him like her own. Attached to this letter is a copy of my will. You will see I have left every-

thing to you. I know now that Scottie will be okay, and you and Sabela will raise him right. Maybe someday, you can read the letter I wrote to him.

Hold him tight and tell him his mommy loves him.

Eve

My body shook and I couldn't ever remember crying as hard as I was at this moment. I buried my head into the crook of Sabela's shoulder. I was a father and didn't know how to handle it. My life would be forever changed and so would Sabela's. We were suddenly parents. I pulled Sabela in close, wrapping my arms around her neck, and I let the tears fall. I wasn't ashamed—this was one of the most emotional times of my life, and I wasn't about to hide the raw feeling I was going through right now. Sabela joined me in my tears, her head buried in my hair.

From across the table, I heard the faint sniffs from Patricia as she wiped her now drenched cheeks. "I'm so sorry, Ian. I had no idea Scottie was yours. I don't think she told anyone. She made us all believe he was David's." She dabbed her eyes. "I haven't seen you in so many years. If I had, I would have seen the resemblance, clearly."

I lifted my head away from Sabela and turned to face Patricia. "Please, Patricia, you should not be apologizing for what Eve has done."

Patricia nodded.

"You've just lost your daughter, and now you are here, picking up the pieces she left behind." Pulling myself together, I left Sabela's side and walked over to Patricia with my arms out.

"I'm so sorry for your loss."

Patricia welcomed my embrace. "Thank you," she said between her sobs. "She was so young. She just had her thirtieth birthday."

"I know. She was my age." My legs were still shaking from the intensity of the shock. "I need to sit down."

Sabela came to my aid and pulled out a chair. She stood behind me, rubbing my shoulders while I asked Patricia another question.

"When can I see him?"

"Tomorrow, if you'd like," she said with pain in her voice. "The house is going to be so quiet without him."

I took Patricia's hand. "I know we've had our differences, but I promise you, Scottie will always be a part of your life. He just lost his mother. He's not going to lose his only grandmother too."

She squeezed my hand. "Thank you," she said with bated breath.

I looked up at Sabela, who was still standing behind me, her hands resting on my shoulders. Dealing with the shock, I hadn't said much to her. "How are you doing? Are you okay?" I asked, while taking her hand.

"Yes, I'm okay. I just can't believe it. You're a dad."

"Sabela, you will be his new mom. Are you okay with that?"

I knew as soon as she knelt beside me and took my face in her hands and wept, that she was. "Slater, what kind of a silly question is that? He's your son. He is a part of you. I would be honored to be his mother and together we will do the best we can on raising him."

Tears trickled down my cheeks as she spoke. I kissed her gently on the lips. "I love you so much."

"I love you too. Who knows, maybe someday we'll give him a brother or sister."

For the first time since the shocking news broke, I smiled. "You bet we will."

CHAPTER 22

SABELA

Slater didn't have to ask me if I wanted to be Scottie's new mother. I didn't care that he was Eve's child. Scottie needed a mother and my heart was already heaving from the thought we were now his parents. I couldn't wait to meet him and hold him in my arms.

After learning about the shocking news, it was Patricia's turn to talk. Her heart was broken from losing her youngest daughter at such a young age. I had sat next to Patricia, holding her in my arms while she broke down and wept. She had lost her husband twenty years ago, never remarried, and raised her two girls on her own. Now it was just she and Eve's sister, Lorraine. Again, both Slater and I promised Scottie would continue to be a big part of their lives.

We listened as Patricia spoke through her continued heart-wrenching sobs and broken voice, about the day Eve called and told her about the terminal cancer. "We must have cried for hours together on the phone that day," Patricia said, wiping her eyes with her now damp tissue.

"Do you want some tea?" I asked her, rubbing her shoulders.

"Yes, please."

Slater didn't drink tea. "Do you want a beer?" I asked him.

"Yeah, that would be great."

I left the table and listened from the kitchen while Patricia told us what she knew.

"I knew she wasn't happy with that man. I guess you could say it was a mother's intuition."

I nodded, not wanting to interrupt her, while placing a tea bag in one of the cups I had set out on the counter.

Patricia had our full attention and continued to speak. "Eve had confessed to me about her awful marriage to David. They had been married for just over three years, and Scottie had just turned three. During that time, David had only seen Scottie maybe three times." Patricia shook her head in disgust. "Can you believe that?"

"What a jerk," I said, placing a beer in front of Slater and a cup of tea by Patricia.

"Thank you," Patricia said before taking a welcomed sip.

I heard the beer can being popped open as I returned to the kitchen to retrieve my cup of tea.

Slater guzzled his beer and smacked his lips. "Thanks, I needed that."

Once we were all seated back at the table—this time, I sat next to Slater and took his hand—Patricia told us some more.

She thought for a moment. "Where was I? Oh, yes. He saw Scottie, one time for a publicity stunt, when he was three months old. The other two times were also photo opportunities. Once she was diagnosed, she never told David, and insisted on a quick divorce settlement.

"When she told him he would have no obligations when it came to Scottie, he didn't hesitate, and she walked away with ten million. Honestly, I'm surprised he married her at all but knowing my Eve, she probably threatened to tarnish his image if he didn't. She immediately came back to California and bought the house in Del Mar, and told me she wanted to make it perfect for Scottie."

"Ten million." I gasped while looking over at Slater, who didn't seem fazed by the amount.

Patricia nodded. "Yes. He basically paid her off to leave him alone." Patricia's eyes narrowed. "And I don't care what you think, she deserved every cent for the way he treated her," she said in a defensive tone.

Neither Slater nor I dared to argue with her and listened as she continued telling us some more.

"Within a week of buying the house, she brought Scottie to come stay with me." She took in a deep breath. "She was going to start treatment for the tumor. They told her it was inoperable but radiation treatments would slow down the growth. I guess, a few months later, she found you, and her plan was to leave everything perfect for Scottie. She wanted to make sure he would be taken care of and would have everything he ever needed."

At a loss for words and probably emotionally drained, Slater remained silent while Patricia told us the entire story.

"How could she keep this from me for years?" he said, trying to keep back the tears that were now pooling in his eyes.

"In her mind, Slater, Eve honestly thought she was doing the right thing. She was only thinking of Scottie. She didn't think how this would affect you," Patricia said, reaching across the table for Slater's hand.

Slater pushed her hand away and with one abrupt move, shoved his chair back from the table and stood. His face became tight as he spat his words at Patricia. "I lost four years of my son's life because of what she thought was the right thing to do."

I reached for Slater's arm to calm the storm I could see beginning but he brushed me off too and began pacing around the room. "I should have been there for his birth!" he cried. "She had no right to keep that from me."

Slater's emotions were turning to anger. His face was now

flushed. His nostrils were flared, and I was afraid he would say something to Patricia he may regret. I turned to Patricia.

"Maybe you should go. We'll call you in the morning, after we've had a chance to let all this soak in, and arrange to come and meet Scottie."

In an outburst, Slater directed his anger toward me." What do you mean, meet him? He's coming home with us. I'm not going to miss another day with my son."

"Slater, we have nothing here for him. We need to prepare this place for him."

He paced around the room again while he spoke, his hands in the back pockets of his jeans. "We'll buy a bed tomorrow and make room in the office."

"But, Slater, he needs time to adjust. He has just lost his mother and the only person he knows is Patricia."

"No. Slater is right," Patricia butted in, surprising me. "You're his parents now. He needs to get to know you. No sense in procrastinating. The sooner he's with you, the better."

Even though I was outnumbered, I wasn't convinced it was such a good idea. "Don't you think he should ease into this transition? He's only four years old."

Slater was shaking his head before I had finished. "Which is exactly why he should come to us as soon as possible. He's young and will adjust quickly," he said, his voice now a little calmer. Seeing my uncertainties, he approached me and rubbed my shoulders. "It's the right thing to do. Trust me on this. Okay?"

I nodded, but I still wasn't convinced. I understood Slater's reasoning. I guess my emotions were running with Scottie, wondering how he was holding up, and then to be told he would be living with two people he doesn't even know... How does a little boy handle that?

Patricia stood and picked up her purse. "Well, you have a lot to talk about." She slid an envelope to the middle of the table. "I will leave these with you to sign. They are papers regarding the will and the keys to Eve's house." She glanced over at Slater. "It's yours now, Slater."

Slater gave a silent nod and quickly turned his head away. He didn't comment on the house. "Thank you. I'll have them signed before I meet with you tomorrow. Can I call you in the morning and arrange a time?"

"That will be fine, I will have Scottie ready for you."

After Patricia left, I went to the fridge to grab a beer. I sure needed one. "Do you want one?" I asked Slater.

But his mind was somewhere else and he didn't answer me. "Slater?" I asked again.

"I don't want the house. And I don't want her money either."

This didn't come as a surprise to me, and I took a seat next to him and popped open my beer. "Do you want to talk about it?"

He looked over at me, and his eyes were sad. "Would you be upset if I didn't take any of it. All I want is Scottie. He's mine, nothing else is."

I took his hand and held it close to my heart. "Oh, sweetheart. I could never be upset with you, especially through a time like this. What you're saying makes sense to me. Whatever you decide, I will support you, one hundred percent. Like I've always said, we're in this together."

Slater strained to break a subtle smile but managed. "Thanks. I love you." He leaned back in his chair, still holding my hand. "I want to raise Scottie the right way. Teach him values, and if he works hard in this world, he will be rewarded. I've worked hard all my life, and when something good happens in my life, I know I've earned it."

I gave him an understanding smile. "I agree with you."

"I don't want him to grow up with a silver spoon in his mouth and given everything on a silver platter. That's Eve's way of raising him, not mine." He released a chuckle. "Shit, when I was with her, she was always looking for the easy way out in life. She never once tried to find a real job where she had to leave the house. She just played around with stupid Internet businesses. But they take a lot of work to get going off the ground, and Eve didn't have it in her to do that. For her, that was too much work." He laughed and shook his head while throwing himself back against the chair. "I can see why she took off with the real estate tycoon—how could she resist? It's what she'd always wanted. Someone to take care of her."

"That sounds about right," I agreed. "Whether you like it or not though, the house and whatever money she has is yours."

"We are not going to live in that house, I can tell you that right now. It's not us. And I'll be damned if I live in some house that I didn't work for. And that goes for her money too. Both you and I have worked hard. We've managed to save quite a bit of money in the bank from what Eve has paid us. It's honest money that we've earned. We probably have enough to put a down payment on a house, don't you think?"

"Yes, we do," I said with a smile.

"I want us to buy our house, not have one handed to us. Does that make sense? Are you okay with all of this?"

I took his other hand, then held them both up to my lips and kissed them tenderly. "It makes a lot of sense. I wouldn't want it any other way."

Slater gave me a loving smile. "What do you say we give the house and her money to The Children of America Fund?"

I knew Slater's heart was big, but this gesture showed me just how big it was. "I think it's a beautiful idea," I replied with tears in my eyes.

"Good. Maybe they can turn the house into a children's home. We will look into it after the will has been finalized. Tomorrow, we'll go by the house and maybe pick up a few things for Scottie that he may like, and then we'll leave the rest there for other children to enjoy."

With tears streaming down my face, I cupped his face in my hands and kissed him softly. "You are an amazing man, Slater. I'm so lucky to have you, and I know you will be a wonderful father to *our* child, Scottie."

He kissed me back. "And you are going to be the most amazing mother. I love you."

"I love you too."

CHAPTER 23

It was two o'clock in the morning and I was still awake, but I wasn't surprised. The sound of Sabela's faint breathing as she slept soundly next to me in my arms was soothing while I still tried to wrap my head around the fact that I was a father. In a matter of twenty-four hours, my life had completely changed. I now had a title—I was a dad. I was now responsible for someone else's life. What I teach him and what he learns from me would affect him for the rest of his life. The realization was mind-blowing but at the same time, liberating. I now had a purpose in life, and that was to raise Scottie the best way I could. Instill in him the values I believed in and set a good example for him. Those were my last thoughts before I finally drifted off to sleep.

The next morning, still feeling hungover by the news and with very little sleep, Sabela and I went over Eve's will with copious amounts of coffee. It was pretty straightforward, with no complications. Like Patricia said, she had left nearly everything to me and had also set up a trust fund for Scottie. Our decisions had not changed. Once the will was settled, which could take up to a year, everything would be donated. In the meantime, we would maintain the house.

"Are you nervous about meeting Scottie?" Sabela asked, sitting next to me on the couch with her third cup of coffee in her hand.

I didn't need to think about my answer. "Actually, no, I'm not. I'm excited more than anything. I want us to be a family as soon as possible."

"I'm excited too." She picked up her phone from the coffee table and checked the time. "Do you want to get dressed and head over to Eve's house to pick up some things?"

"Let me make some phone calls first. I need to call Travis. We're going to finish the job over there, but I'm going to put Travis in charge. What do you think?" I didn't wait for her answer. "I think it would be a good idea if we took some time off, and just spent all of our time with Scottie, so he can get to know us and feel comfortable."

Sabela smiled and stroked my thigh through my sweats. "I think that's a great idea. I was going to suggest something like that," she said before standing. "I'm going to get dressed and leave you to make your calls." She turned to face me before walking away. "Oh, don't forget to call Patricia and let her know what time we'll be at her house."

"It's on my list." I smiled.

It took me a few hours to make all the necessary phone calls. The call to Travis took the longest, since I needed to explain to him why I was suddenly making him chief. *"Wow, man!"* Those were his first words after I told him. *"You're a dad. Damn, everything makes sense now. We all suspected Eve was hiding something. I just didn't think it would be your kid,"* he had added. After the initial shock of learning about my newfound fatherhood, like the true friend he was, he told me not to worry about the job—he would take care of it.

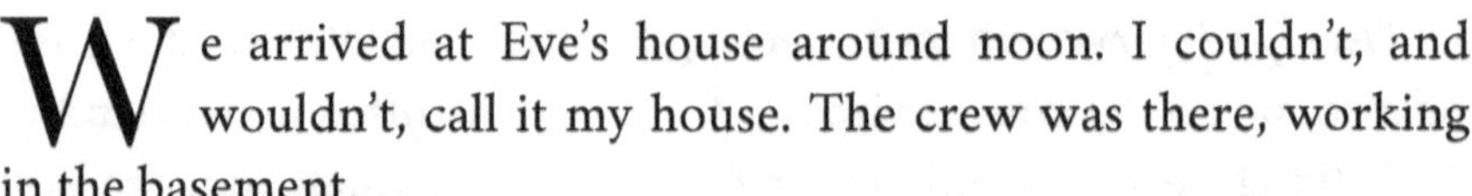

We arrived at Eve's house around noon. I couldn't, and wouldn't, call it my house. The crew was there, working in the basement.

"Hey, I need to go over some things with Travis." I handed Sabela the keys to the house. "Do you want to gather up a few things for Scottie?"

"Sure, I'll see what I can find. She might have some clothes for him someplace, and I'll gather up some toys," she said.

Travis and I spent the next thirty minutes going over what needed to be done to complete the job and afterward, I felt comfortable leaving him in charge. I knew he wouldn't let me down. I shook his hand and gave him a pat on the shoulder. "Thanks, man. I knew I could count on you." I glanced at my watch. "Now, I gotta go find Sabela. We need to get going."

"No problem, man. Hey, try calling her phone."

"Good idea." I laughed and pulled my phone out of my back pocket.

Sabela didn't answer her phone, so I began checking every one of the many rooms. When I reached the top of the stairs, I saw the master bedroom door was open. It had always been locked. There must have been a key on the set I gave Sabela. Unsure what to expect, I approached the room with caution.

When I walked through the doorway, chills swept over me. I was entering the personal space of a woman who was no longer there but all her belongings were. All the drapes were closed, and the room was dimly lit by a small lamp on the nightstand.

I found Sabela sitting on the edge of the bed, holding a picture frame, while she traced the image with her fingers. She looked my way, and it was then I saw the tears streaming down her face.

I rushed to her side. "Sabela. Are you okay?"

She handed me the frame. "It's your son," she cried.

I took the picture and saw the image of a little boy sitting on the same bed we were, holding a white teddy bear. He looked identical to me. I couldn't stop looking at it. Every detail—his eyes, his chin, his nose, hair, and his hands. "My god, he looks just like me."

Sabela's tears didn't let up. "I know, and look, his picture is everywhere."

I pulled my eyes away from the photo and glanced around the room—there must have been ten or more pictures of Scottie. I handed Sabela the frame in my hand and slowly rose from the bed. I walked over to each picture, picking up every one and studying every little detail. These were images of the times I had missed with my son, from when he was a newborn until today.

"We're taking these," I said, gathering them up in my arms.

Sabela sniffed back her tears and took them from me. "I'll put them in with the bag of clothes I've gathered for Scottie."

I nodded while staring at a picture of my son wrapped in a blanket, his eyes barely open. "This must have been when he was born." I traced the outline of his face with my finger. "I should have been there," I said, handing it to Sabela.

"You didn't know, Slater. You would have been if you did." She placed the picture in the bag with the others. "I have another bag in the hallway with some toys for him, and I also packed a box with bedding and blankets."

"Good." I walked toward the door of the master bath. "Have you been in here yet?" I asked as I opened the door and went in.

Sabela followed me in. "No not yet, I got distracted by the pictures."

"Look at all this. No wonder she kept the door locked," I said in a whisper, shocked by what I was seeing. Both Sabela and I stood in the middle of the room, looking at the line of wigs perched on the counter. There must have been a dozen of them—all different colors, ranging from jet black, blonde, and fiery red, each on their own stand. A basket of medicines sat in front of them, mostly for pain.

"I recognize that blonde one from when I first met her," Sabela said. "She must have had no hair because of the treatment she was going through."

"That, or it was really short," I suggested. "She didn't want us to see any of this, and especially the pictures of Scottie."

"I can see why. There's no doubt he is your son."

I took Sabela's hand and swung it gently in mine. "Speaking of which, let's go meet him and bring him home," I said, before kissing her lips.

After telling the guys we were leaving and loading the truck with Scottie's things, I made a quick call to Patricia to let her know we were on our way, and that we should be there in an hour. She told me they were ready for us.

It was the longest drive of my life. Sabela and I did a lot of talking to keep our nerves at bay. My biggest concern was how Scottie would react. I didn't want him to be afraid of me, I wanted him to trust me. But how do you tell that to a four-year-old child? Sabela told me I wouldn't have to. She believed Scottie would just know. God, I hoped she was right.

When we pulled up outside Patricia's house—which looked like every other house in the neighborhood, except the floor plans had been switched around—I let the truck run idle for a few minutes while I stared at the front door from inside the cab.

Sabela rubbed my thigh. "Are you okay?" she asked.

"My son is on the other side of that door. Right now, we are a couple, and when we come back out that door, we will be parents. That is some really heavy shit to take in. It just hit me. *Bam!*"

"I know. It all seems so real, all of a sudden. Are you ready to go meet your son?" Sabela asked, her hand on the door handle.

I turned off the truck and took the keys out of the ignition. "As ready as I'll ever be," I replied, stepping out of the truck and putting the keys in my back pocket.

Hand in hand, we walked up to the front door and rang the bell. I took a deep breath and squeezed Sabela's hand tight. She squeezed mine back. A few minutes later, the door opened. Even though I'd not seen her in a few years, I recognized her to be Eve's sister, Lorraine. Her hair was still its original light-brown color, long past her shoulders, and straight. She had gained a few pounds, but on her tall frame, she no longer looked skinny, which was how I remembered her. She was dressed causal in jeans and a red t-shirt.

"Hi, Lorraine."

"Hi, Ian. Come on in," she replied, opening the door wider to let us through.

Still holding onto Sabela's hand, we entered the home. It was quiet except for the faint sound of a television coming from the other end of the house.

"He's in the den with my mom. Follow me," Lorraine said.

My heart was racing as we followed her down the hallway. I could feel the stickiness between Sabela's hand and mine as our palms became sweaty. The sound of the television grew louder as we approached the closed door of the den.

Lorraine turned to face us. "Are you ready?" she asked.

"Does he know we're coming, and does he know who I am?"

Lorraine shook her head. "No, not yet. He wouldn't understand without you being here."

I nodded. "Ahh, okay. Then yes, I'm ready."

I watched as Lorraine turned the handle to the door where my son was. Anticipating his reaction, and with a huge breath, I entered the room. I saw him immediately. His back was facing us. He was sitting on the floor, watching cartoons on the television. Patricia was by his side, sitting in a recliner. Neither one knew we were in the room until Lorraine spoke.

"Mom, they're here."

Patricia strained her neck and turned to face us. Removing her glasses, she rose to her feet and walked around Scottie to greet us.

"Hello, Ian," she said, shaking my hand.

"Come here." I let go of Sabela's hand to embrace Patricia. "We have to stick together for Scottie. You are part of my family now because you are my son's grandmother."

Patricia smiled. "Thank you, that means a lot." She then turned and walked over to Scottie, who was mesmerized by whatever show was on. She turned it off and extended her hand to him. "Scottie, there's someone here to meet you."

Scottie looked up to her and took her hand, while standing to his feet. I noticed, in his other hand, he was holding the teddy bear from the picture. He turned and looked at me, and I couldn't stop the tears from falling. Sabela wrapped her arm around my waist and whispered in my ear, "He's beautiful."

"Hello, Scottie," I said, slowly walking toward him and holding on to Sabela for strength, afraid my legs would cave in from under me.

He smiled, which instantly melted my heart, and said, "Hello."

I knelt before him and looked into his eyes, feeling the soft hand of Sabela on my shoulder as I met my son for the first time. He was perfect in every way, and looked every bit like me, from the color of his hair and eyes, to his cheekbones, and even his nose. When he smiled, I saw my smile.

He held his teddy bear by one arm, letting it dangle beside him. "Why are you crying?" he asked.

I sniffed through my tears and chuckled. Why are kids always so curious? "They are tears of joy because I'm meeting you for the first time." I looked at his bear. "Who is your friend?"

Scottie pulled him up and hugged him. "This is Snowy."

"That's a great name. Do you know who I am?"

He shook his head.

I took one of his small hands and looked him in the eyes. "I'm your daddy."

Scottie looked at me, a puzzled look on his face. "You are? I've never had a daddy before."

I smiled, tears still gushing down my face. "Well, you have one now. Can I have a hug, buddy?"

"Okay," Scottie said, and he opened his arms while still holding on to Snowy with one.

At that very moment, I felt a love I had never experienced before. It was different from the love I felt for Sabela. This was a fatherly love that touched me in ways I couldn't even begin to describe. As I held my son gently in my arms, I knew I was going to be the best person I could ever be for him, with the help of Sabela.

"Hey, do you want to meet someone else?" I asked, while he was still curled in my arms.

"Okay."

I unwrapped my arms from him and took Sabela's hand. She knelt beside us and gave Scottie a loving smile. "Hi, Scottie."

Scottie gave her a smile. "Hi."

I took Scottie's hand. "This is Sabela. She's going to be my wife soon, which means she would be your mommy. Is that okay?"

"My mommy's gone. Will she be my new mommy?"

I knew he didn't understand what had happened to Eve, and probably didn't know he would never see her again. In time, he would learn what happened. "Yes, she can be your new mommy. Do you want to give her hug too?"

I watched as the two people who meant more to me than anything embraced for the first time, and then I joined them in a family hug. "I love you guys," I whispered.

"We love you too," Sabela said through her tears.

Pulling myself together, I rose to my feet and took Scottie's hand. "Hey, do you have any games we could play together?"

Scottie eyed lit up and his smile grew wide. "I have some Legos. Will you build something with me?"

"Of course. Can you go get them?"

For the next few hours, Sabela and I played and read books

with Scottie. We took him for a walk around the neighborhood, each of us holding a hand and swinging him in the air.

"Again!" He would scream and laugh every time his feet touched the ground.

When we returned to the house, Patricia had lunch ready. Over our meal, I knew I had to ask Scottie the big question. As I sat next to him, I put my hand on his shoulder. "Hey, Scottie, how would you like to come live with me and your new mommy?"

He chewed on a French fry as he spoke. "Can Grandma come too?"

"No, Scottie, I have my own house here, and you can come visit whenever you want. Your room will still be here, with all your toys." I looked over at Patricia and smiled, relieved she answered his question.

I held my breath, waiting to see what Scottie would say next. I watched as he put another fry in his mouth and then picked up his bear from his lap. "Can Snowy come too?"

Tears wallowed in my eyes. "Of course Snowy can come. We can even get him a friend, if you'd like."

Scottie's eyes lit up. "Really?"

I laughed. "Yes, really."

"Snowy would like that."

"So, what do you say, kiddo? Do you and Snowy want to come live with us?"

Scottie grinned, which caused his fry to fall out of his mouth. "Yes, we do."

"That's my boy." I pulled him in and held him close, then looked over at Sabela, who was also crying. "Is that okay with you, Mommy? That Scottie comes live with us."

Sabela spoke through her tears. "I would love it."

With our son between us, chewing on another French fry, I reached behind him and took Sabela's hand. "I think it's about time Mommy and Daddy plan a wedding and make this family official. Don't you?"

Sabela kissed the top of my hand as I gave her a loving smile. "I do."

ABOUT THE AUTHOR

Tina Hogan Grant loves to write stories with strong female characters that know what they want and aren't afraid to chase their dreams. She loves to write sexy and sometimes steamy romances with happy ever after endings.

She is living life to the fullest in a small mountain community in Southern California with her husband and two dogs. When she is not writing she is probably riding her ATV, kayaking or hiking with her best friend – her husband of twenty-five years.

www.tinahogangrant.com

WHERE CAN YOU FIND TINA?

Join her Facebook Reading Group where she does live chats, cover reveals, reads excerpts and does plenty of giveaways including signed ACR books.

FOLLOW HER ON THESE SOCIAL MEDIA ACCOUNTS